THE AUDACIOUS HIGHWAYMAN

When Sophie once again meets her childhood hero Julian, who's been sent home in disgrace, she feels that romance has made her life complete. However, her brother Tom and his friend Harry must confine Sophie to her home because highwaymen have been sighted in the area. Sophie, contemptuous of the highwayman rumours, finds that any secret assignation with Julian seems doomed to failure. Then — when she's involved in a frightening encounter with the highwayman — her life is changed for ever.

Books by Beth James
in the Linford Romance Library:

IT STARTED WITH A KISS
UNBREAK MY HEART
THE SILVER VINAIGRETTE
OUT OF REACH
STRANGERS IN THE NIGHT

BETH JAMES

THE AUDACIOUS HIGHWAYMAN

Complete and Unabridged

LINFORD
Leicester

First published in Great Britain in 2010

First Linford Edition
published 2011

British Library CIP Data

James, Beth.
  The audacious highwayman. - -
  (Linford romance library)
  1. Brigands and robbers- -Fiction.
  2. Love stories. 3. Large type books.
  I. Title II. Series
  823.9'2–dc22

  ISBN 978–1–4448–0767–7

Published by
F. A. Thorpe (Publishing)
Anstey, Leicestershire

Set by Words & Graphics Ltd.
Anstey, Leicestershire
Printed and bound in Great Britain by
T. J. International Ltd., Padstow, Cornwall

This book is printed on acid-free paper

1

'Actually, dashed if she ain't such a bad proposition after all,' pronounced Tom Ellington, appraising his sister as she stood framed against the light of the library casement window.

'Not at all,' agreed Tom's friend Harry, an attractive smile lighting up his otherwise quite commonplace features. 'Engaging little thing. Always thought so.'

'Yes,' Tom went on, circling round Sophie. 'Nice neat form, pleasant manners, good teeth.'

Sophie gritted her 'good' teeth, and straightened her 'nice, neat' form. 'Beg pardon, but will you cease discussing me as though I were a horse.'

Harry threw back his head and laughed, while Tom put a finger to his chin as though re-assessing the situation. 'Maybe I was wrong about the manners . . . Trifle too spirited a filly perhaps. And then there's the freckles — forgot all about those.'

'They've gone now,' Sophie said indignantly. 'Anyway, yours are worse, and your hair is red, whereas mine is pale auburn — much more acceptable.'

'With that, I have to comply,' Harry said with a gravity belied by the twinkle in his eye.

Tom ruffled a careless hand through his dark, red curls. 'Yes,' he admitted cheerfully. 'Perhaps my hair will be a problem. Pity the powdered wig is so outmoded now, I might have cut quite a dash in a powdered wig and satin knee breeches. I wonder why it is that young ladies of fashion, particularly well bred, rich, ladies of fashion, abhor red hair. What's your advice?' he asked turning to Harry.

A smile was never far from Harry's open, good-humoured face. 'Keep your hat on, my friend. Keep your hat on.'

'At all times?'

'At all times,' Sophie agreed with a

triumphant smile.

'Perchance a little eccentric at social occasions? At a ball for example?'

'Well, at least until you get to know the lady heiress,' Harry advised.

'And how do I do that, with my hat stuck firmly on my head? Have to take it off when I make my introductory bow, surely?'

'You meet her on horseback of course. Even you can pass muster on horseback; you have a good seat, a charming smile and a mysterious air of recklessness about you . . . Yes, that's an excellent notion.' Sophie warmed to her theme. 'You rescue her when she's in peril. You save her life, when her horse has bolted!'

'Eh? And how do I achieve that, pray?'

'Oh you're both so clever, I'm sure you can contrive something,' Sophie said airily. 'Anyhow, freckles or no freckles, brother of mine, I don't have to vex myself too much over making an advantageous marriage. I've always got the sapphire necklace.'

'Ah,' said Harry.

'Ah,' said Tom.

'What d'you mean — 'ah'?'

Tom scratched the side of his aristocratic-looking nose. 'Didn't want to mention it, but you might as well know, Lord Horton has already sold the Rubens and some of the best plate. Heaven knows when he might take the notion to sell the necklace.'

The smile died from Sophie's eyes and she sat down rather suddenly. 'But it's mine,' she said. 'Bequeathed to me as part of my dowry, from my mother's side not my father's. My stepfather surely cannot touch it. He can't, can he, Harry? You must know about these things.'

Uncomfortably, Harry ran a finger round the inside edge of his cravat. 'In theory no, of course, he can't ... Unfortunately, in practice, with his gambling friends dunning for payment, it's a different story. The trade now, they could be put off, but your mother wouldn't do that. Not her style. Decent type, Lady Horton . . . At any event, gambling debts are altogether more pressing — matter of honour.'

Sophie bit her lip. Suddenly, the conversation did not feel so amusing. So this was why, when she'd stumbled upon the two men in the library, deep in a discussion concerning the Ellington's future fortune, they'd turned it into a matter for jest. They thought to spare her sensibilities.

'I see,' she said slowly. 'Things are worse then than I feared. So exactly when were you going to tell me all this?'

The set expression of her brother and the steady, open gaze of his friend, were answer enough. 'I comprehend you were out to spare my finer feelings. Well, no matter. I know now and I am not the type of female to go into vapours, you know that I am not. I'm glad that I understand now that this is indeed serious and you and I, Tom, are duty bound to make beneficial marriages.'

'No need to look so glum,' Tom said. 'Felix might have a run of luck at the tables, pay off all his debts and retire to Ellington Park never to gamble again. I might meet a ravishing beauty who becomes besotted with me and turns out to be an heiress to boot. Harry's Aunt Augustine might die and leave her fortune to him — then he could marry you.'

'Glad to oblige,' Harry put in at this point.

But Sophie was not to be diverted. 'Pray, what was it that brought this discussion about? Has something lately happened to make the matter suddenly more pressing?'

Tom met her eyes squarely, then sighed. 'Well, if you must have it. It's Mama,' he said softly. 'She's worried for my inheritance. You know there are another eighteen months before I am five and twenty and have full control over the estate, and she would like to see it pass to me intact. I beg you don't tease her with this, because although she didn't say, I know she won't want your knowledge of it. I came upon her by accident, poring over the household accounts, seeking ways of economy. Since then I have had meetings with the estate manager of our home.

'Things ain't as they should be. We performed a secret inventory and as I said, it seems the Rubens is suddenly become a mere copy and some of the family plate missing. It's a shocking business but unfortunately all too common when a rich widow such as Mama marries a hardened gamester like Felix.'

'And did you notice this, Harry? I must confess, having lived here all my life, I have missed neither the silver plate or the Rubens.'

'Well,' Harry said, returning her gaze steadily, 'the Rubens was copied, probably under guise of being cleaned. We're sure that the one hanging in the long gallery is a fake. The real one has probably been sold abroad.'

Sophie's heart sank. 'But that's

terrible, Harry. What's to stop him copying the necklace, and selling the real sapphires?'

'He could only do that with Mama's consent,' said Tom. 'She mainly wears it in London, only for the very best social occasions. It's usually lodged in the City Bank, where they would only give it up to her in person, for it is highly valuable, as you know. And when she brings it here it's kept in our secret hiding place behind the panelling.' Tom indicated the far wall that was lined with books. 'Only you and I and Mama know where exactly — so it's safe enough here.'

'But Lord Horton and our mother are in London at the present. What's to stop him forcing her . . . ' Thinking of her charming but weak stepfather, Sophie broke off.

'Never fret, Sophie. Felix won't really do that. As long as there are horses in the stable, silk carpets, and plate, Mama will stand firm about the necklace.'

'And then?'

'And by that time, we will have found a way out of all this. Poor prospects or not.' His serious expression lightening a little, Tom turned to his friend. 'Now come on Harry, let's talk about you for a change. How are things with the law?'

'Studying the law, is a necessary bore,' Harry said rhyming couplet style. 'But alas, my marriage prospects are dismal.'

''Fraid so,' agreed Tom. 'Utterly abysmal. Even that wet Julian Stafford-Smythe is the son of a Baron. Poor Harry, with a father who's a man of the cloth, has nothing to recommend him at all.'

At the mention of Julian's name, Sophie turned away in order to hide the faint blush that stole into her cheeks at the mere thought of him. Although she had not seen Julian Stafford-Smythe these last six months, rarely did a day go past without him entering her thoughts. With his coal black hair, pale skin and dark violet eyes, he was the romantic figure to outclass all others, and ever since their first meeting back in their childhood years, Sophie had always felt there was an empathy between them.

Not so Harry and Tom, who could never understand that just because a person didn't take an interest in the country pursuits of hunting and fishing, he needn't be judged as a town toff and dreadful bore into the bargain.

'Oh I'm sure Julian can't be as wet as he was,' Harry said. However the look of gratitude that Sophie shot him soon faded as he added, 'I'm persuaded he couldn't be! He must have grown up a little.'

'I'd not be tempted to a wager on it,' countered Tom. 'It would be difficult indeed. Always mooning about, waffling on about trees and flowers and broken hearts. Enough to make a man cast up his accounts.'

'You exaggerate,' Sophie butted in, no longer able to hear her hero discussed in such disparaging terms.

'He's a romantic and he was very much in love the last time we saw him . . . Calf love, Mama said. He's very likely over that now and back to his senses.'

Her brother cast his eyes up to the beautiful Adam-style ceiling. 'Doubtful if he ever had any. Always a milk sop if you ask me. Traipsing round the countryside quoting poetry. Queer in the upper storey, I'd say!'

'Well, no matter,' Harry said, nevertheless giving Sophie a scrutinising glance. 'He may be the son of a baron, but he's as near penury as I. Closer, I'd say — so no fortune to be had there, I'm afraid, Sophie.'

'At any event,' Tom interrupted, 'you're not queer in your attic. You may be a man of letters, and have a head for business. Never seen you prancing about spouting poetry though, like Stafford-Smythe. That I couldn't abide.'

'I find this conversation unpleasant,' Sophie said, crossing back to the window and staring out at the extensive

11

Ellington parklands beyond. 'Unpleasant and distasteful. We know the situation, I see no need to discuss it further . . . ' She swung back round to face them. 'And look, it's quite clear outside now, so why don't we take that ride you suggested earlier, Tom?'

'Yes,' Tom said, brightening up immediately. 'At least, Harry and I will. You shouldn't come, Sophie; you'll only want to turn back as soon as it begins to rain.'

Typical Tom, Sophie thought. *Always the bossy elder brother.*

The trouble with Tom was, he had no soul; no wonder he didn't appreciate the finer sentiments of a man like Julian Stafford-Smythe.

'I'll come if I want to. Mama allows me to ride unaccompanied on the estate — you know it, so I will be no inconvenience to you if I can't keep up. Anyway, it's not going to rain, that's obvious to anyone who knows anything at all about the weather.'

Harry and Tom exchanged glances

before following her out of the library to change their boots for the stables.

★ ★ ★

Three-quarters of an hour later however, mist had descended, some heavy-bellied clouds had rolled across and the first few spots of rain were making themselves felt.

Sophie wiped a splash of mud from the side of her elegant nose and gently kicked Apple Pie's nether regions with her well-booted heel. Harry and Tom were two small specks in the misty distance by now and she knew she had no real hope of catching them. As was usual, they'd mounted her on the oldest, laziest mare in the stable.

'You're the one who insists on keeping Apple Pie, even though she's no use any more. So you're the one to exercise her — obviously,' Tom had said in his usual elder-brother fashion.

'Shush she'll hear you, she's sensitive,' Sophie answered. 'Anyway, I didn't say I wouldn't ride her, just that it would make a pleasant change to ride a more lively mount — like Firefly, perhaps, or even Prince of Thieves.'

'Tell you what, Sophie, you can ride Regency Buck tomorrow,' Harry interjected before Tom could tell her that she wasn't capable of riding either horse. 'You'll like him. He's nippy in the field but very gentle. My sister would be pleased if you exercised him while she's away, I know it.'

Tom shot Harry a sceptical glance. 'Wouldn't do that. Sophie's not an out and outer in the saddle like Lizzie. She's not halfway firm enough. That's why Apple Pie's so lazy. It's all Sophie's own doing . . . '

Thinking of this previous conversation now, Sophie sniffed and wished that Tom wasn't always so very right. He'd been right when he said it would rain. Right when he'd pointed out that they would lose her within half a mile and she needn't think they'd wait for her, and right when he'd said he couldn't see the point in her coming anyway, when she knew she couldn't keep up and hated riding in the rain.

Dejectedly, Sophie turned Apple Pie towards the old barn, intending to shelter there until the worst of the weather had passed over. The somewhat dilapidated building had served as their childhood playground and nestled snugly in the curve of the hill. Should Tom and Harry miss her, which she doubted very much, they would be sure to know to look for her there.

Having reached the shelter she dismounted with a graceful ease, which even her brother would not dispute, and prepared to spend an uncomfortable period sitting on a prickly bale of straw, contemplating a doleful future. As Sophie saw it, her future would be either with a husband she hated and enough money to be comfortable, or a husband she could at least respect, even like, but living in poor circumstances to which she was entirely unused. Or perhaps, failing this delightful prospect,

15

a career as a governess, which she could not think she would find at all agreeable.

Sophie sighed, then started as she heard her sigh echoed.

She peered into the depths of the gloomy barn. 'Who's there?' she called in a voice in which she was distressed to hear a quaver.

'Only the most miserable man in Christendom.'

'Oh,' Sophie replied because there seemed to be no other answer. Then, as a shadow detached itself from the far wall. 'J-J-Julian? Is that you?'

'Unfortunately, yes, 'tis I . . . More's the pity.'

The light slanted through the door bathing him in an ethereal glow as he wearily came towards her.

Sophie thought she might faint, but because she wasn't prone to fainting and also didn't want to miss even a second of this interesting scenario, she remained upright and smiled a wide friendly smile. 'Oh, come on, Julian;

whatever it is, it surely cannot be so very terrible.'

Julian extended a pale, languid hand. 'If you do not consider it so very terrible to be cast off by one's friends, by one's family, and have one's entire life in utter ruins, then no, perhaps it is not. But my dear Sophie — it is Sophie, is it not? — My dear Sophie, I have to tell you my spirits are sorely at a stand and truly I do not exaggerate when I say to you that many times this last month I have wished myself to be without life, to end this purgatory.'

'Oh, never say so,' rejoined Sophie. 'That is a wicked thing to say. I am sure when you have thought about it, you will want to retract that sentiment. We all feel down sometimes. Inclement weather can bring strange notions.'

'Inclement weather?' Julian repeated, faintly.

'Yes,' Sophie said firmly. 'Why even I, and I have a very sensible disposition, anyone will tell you, even I feel a little despondent. Thinking about the future

17

and how little control I have over it. But you are a man; you are able to do whatever you please.'

Julian's violet eyes looked deep into hers for a powerful moment. Then he raked his long sensitive fingers through his carefully tousled black hair. 'Ah, Sophie, Sophie. You are so young, so very young. What can you know about my troubles?'

As though he could no longer bear the weight of his tall, willowy body he sank down on the bale of straw, and rested his head in his hands.

After about a minute in which Sophie had the uncomfortable fear that Julian was indeed on the brink of shedding a tear or two, she could bear it no longer. 'Julian, it can't be true that your family has cast you off without a penny. They would never do so. Anyway, you must still be staying with them or else you'd never be here, in our old barn, would you?'

A strangled sound, that might have been a sob or a snort of amusement, escaped Julian's throat. 'Ah Sophie! Always so prosaic. How fortunate it must be to have such a commonplace humour . . . If only I could be a little more like you.'

Sophie hovered halfway between outrage at being considered to have a commonplace humour and delight at being envied for it by Julian — of all people. 'Well, you have no mount with you, so you must have walked over here from your home; a bare two miles, if you come through the woods, which I would do because it is such a pretty walk at this time of year with the bluebells and the primroses. And you do have a passion for nature and flowers, do you not?'

Julian was staring at her with an expression of sheer disbelief on his face, which Sophie noted but chose to ignore. 'And really,' she went on at a fast pace. 'Really, do you not find it uplifting to smell the bluebells and hear the thrushes and blackbirds in full song? Why it's almost worth feeling

19

miserable for a while, when a mere walk can lift the spirits to such a height so unexpectedly . . . Don't you agree?'

At this, and somewhat to her surprise Julian threw his head back and gave the rasping imitation of a laugh. Sophie smiled triumphantly. As laughs went, it lacked spontaneity and any real amusement, but it was a start.

And a start was all she needed.

2

Rain lashed against the windows and the candles on the table guttered alarmingly. The long mahogany dining table felt over-large to Sophie as with only Tom for company she dined that evening. She had thought to be sharing their meal with Harry, but the weather had grown so inclement that after his ride with Tom, Harry had deemed it wise to return straight to his home at the rectory.

'With Lizzie being away on a visit to Aunt Augustine, I know the old man likes my company,' he had explained to Tom. 'I'd best get back as soon as I possibly can.'

'Can't see why that should be,' replied Tom who looked on Harry as the brother he'd never had and valued his company accordingly. 'Begging your pardon, Harry, but your father only talks about the Greek classics and the like; I don't see how a fellow can have a decent conversation with him.'

Harry only smiled in answer.

'Oh, all right then. I'll own he knows a prodigious amount about fishing and can caste a fly to put the rest of us to shame. And I do see that you must keep the old man company, and I suppose I like you the better for it. But promise me we'll meet up again soon. It can seem confounded dull with no visitors here.'

'No fear of that, Tom. I'll ride over very soon and bring Regency Buck on a leading rein for Sophie. At all events, you should take the opportunity to converse with your estate manager; he's a good fellow and you need to be up to scratch with all Ellington affairs, now we are aware just how far your stepfather is prepared to go.'

A cloud passed over Tom's face. 'Yes indeed,' he agreed. 'I hate all this underhand business, though, it makes me feel like a spy.'

Harry looked at him with sympathy. 'Ellington Park gives you responsibilities, Tom. It's unfortunate that Lord Horton is not a man you can share them with . . . You are not so very alone, though; you have Sophie, whom I know you choose to discount, but who shows a deal of common sense for a girl of only eighteen summers. And of course you know I am always at your service to help you in any way I can.'

Ignoring the stream of water that spilled from the brim of his hat, Tom leaned over in his saddle and clapped Harry on the back prior to his departing. 'You're a dependable fellow, Harry. If only my mother had married someone more like you!'

Harry laughed. 'That would be a fine thing,' he said. 'You and Sophie my stepchildren . . . I cannot comprehend of a worse fate for a young man of five and twenty.' He shuddered as if the thought was too much to be borne and, still laughing, cantered off into the mist.

* * *

'You are strangely silent this evening, brother,' said Sophie as the first covers were removed. 'Did you enjoy your ride in the elements? Didn't catch cold, I trust?'

Tom grinned. 'Nothing we like more than hacking around the countryside,' he said. 'Since when did a drop of rain ever hurt anyone? Except for you, of course. I suppose you would worry that it would spoil your complexion.'

'Never considered it,' mused Sophie, spearing some fish onto her fork. 'But I suppose it might.'

'Well perhaps you should . . . Consider it, I mean. After all, even though you're not a diamond of the first water, I would put you above commonplace and if Mama intends to bring you out next season, you should surely try to preserve any advantages nature has given you.'

Sophie gave him an icy stare. 'As, maybe, should you,' she returned.

'Although, as we mentioned before, there's the red hair to consider — not much to do about that, I warrant.'

'I only meant . . . ' Tom paused. 'All I was trying to say was that, well, Sophie, you're not completely bird-witted, and you must know you're considered to be a good-looking gal.'

'Good-looking gal! . . . Tom, if you are trying to pay me a compliment, please don't; you are making a sorry mess of it and I pity any young lady you do decide to court. If, on the other hand, you are anxious to convey that I must take the idea of making a satisfactory marriage to heart, let me assure you I have, and I will ponder it most seriously.'

Indeed, thought Sophie to herself. She had thought of little else since returning from her chance encounter with Julian. Briefly, she toyed with the notion of confiding in Tom, but no sooner than that idea occurred, than she dismissed it. She already knew Tom and Harry's opinion of Julian.

The knowledge that although he had a comfortable allowance, Julian was not well off and she would never be rich with him, did not give her cause for concern. He was the son of a Baron, and she was sure there would always be a roof for him and his family. At all events, fine clothes and fine houses had never meant so very much to her. Indeed, in their youth, both she and Tom had admitted to feeling more at home in the old rectory with Lizzie and Harry than at Ellington Park with its magnificent reception rooms, galleries and marble staircases. Marriage to Julian would allow her to go on comfortably, in the vicinity of her family home and the same neighbourhood as Harry, Lizzie and her other friends — and of course, she assured herself, she would also be living the fairytale of marriage to a man she truly loved.

Another advantage in marrying Julian would be the non-necessity for an expensive coming-out season in town;

she could take her necklace and what was left of her dowry with her, and there would be one less mouth to feed in Ellington Park. That must surely be an improvement in itself, for hadn't Tom had been known to remark on more than one occasion, that she ate more than all the lads working in the stables put together?

Yes, Sophie thought, *I could happily live without an excess of wealth.*

Love, on the other hand, was something else. Sophie didn't think she could live without love. And she was in love with Julian, of that she was sure.

Of course, at the moment he was in sorely sad spirits. Even his mother had told him to pull himself together and stop pining for a lost love. Indeed, in a way, after listening to a long list of Julian's lost love's attributes, Sophie could almost understand his mother's impatience with him.

Swiftly, Sophie banished this disloyal thought from her mind and conjured up instead the memory of Julian's fine features and brooding violet eyes, as he'd sat with her in the barn discussing the merits of various fashionable poets of the day. He had quoted a few soulful lines to her and she had rapturously hung onto his every word, although it was strange that she could remember none of the quotations now, only the romance of the moment and how truly idyllic the setting was. Well, perhaps not idyllic precisely, but at least it had been private, with no Harry or Tom fidgeting on the sidelines and poking fun behind Julian's back.

Yes, she had been quite content to listen to the resonant timbre of her hero's voice, and drink in the sight of him, with his black tumbled locks, his carelessly tied cravat and his expression of tortured genius. It was quite the most thrilling hour she'd spent since Christmas. And when, at the end of their encounter, Julian had decided it might be prudent for him to start on his long trek back home, she'd volunteered the information that she came riding in this direction, most fine afternoons; he'd glanced back over his shoulder at her and almost smiled. 'Ah, Sophie,' he'd said. 'You are so very sweet. Perhaps you might be able to make my load a little easier to bear.'

Thinking of this now, a small smile hovered round her mouth.

'Don't know what you're looking so moonstruck about,' Tom observed, throwing down his napkin. 'You've a while before Mama brings you out.'

'I know,' said Sophie, snapping herself back to the present and improvising wildly. 'But I will need a new pelisse, many new gowns and hats and bonnets, and I'll be dancing at balls, attending soirées and assemblies and riding on Rotten Row. I was just thinking how agreeable it might be. I'd like a little excitement in my life before I die. If you find life here, stuck in the country so tedious, just imagine how much more so it might be for a girl.'

Tom quaffed down the last of his wine. 'Now why would I do that?

Dashed strange thing to do. Never wanted to be a girl; why should I try to imagine it? Sort of thing Julian would do . . . That reminds me, Wilson, my new valet, tells me Julian's back in the neighbourhood. Been sent back from town, in disgrace.'

'Really?' Sophie said, keeping her eyes downcast. 'Why on earth should that be?'

'Petticoat matter. That's all I'll say about it. Not for your ears, you're my sister after all . . . Oh, and another thing Wilson told me. Highwaymen are back in the area too. Thought we'd seen the last of them, now the law is more vigilant. I'll warrant it's just some hoaxer blowing a trifling robbery out of all proportion, and Wilson swallowing the story whole. Best warn Mama though, when she's home — yes, and Harry too. Not that he's got anything valuable, but some of these ruffians, they'll take a chance, you know. At all events, no more junketing round the neighbourhood on your own. Mama wouldn't like it at all.'

'But Tom, the Highwaymen always stick to the main thoroughfares of Epping, not the farmer's tracks that we are accustomed to use. Anyway, you know you're always too busy to ride with me. You only agreed today in order to appear polite in front of Harry.'

'Take a groom then,' Tom said, unsympathetically. 'And stay round abouts our land.'

'Yes, Tom,' Sophie said, demurely.

Underneath the tabletop, her fingers were firmly crossed.

* * *

Three days later however, when Sophie, the very picture of decorum, was sitting industriously stitching at her embroidery, which had been sadly neglected of late, she was startled to hear a loud-pitched conversation coming from the entrance hall. She recognised her mother's calm tones, interspersed with

31

incredulity, from Mrs Cope the house-keeper, and furious shouting from the usually lazily charming voice of Lord Horton.

Sophie threw down the embroidery with relief and ran to inquire after all the commotion.

'Mama, whatever's to do?'

'Don't fret, my love. We are in fine fettle. No one is hurt, and that is the important thing.'

'But what's amiss?' Sophie asked after running to her mother's arms and kissing her cheek.

'Robbed!' Lord Horton said. 'Dastardly cowards! Stole my fob watch — belonged to my father too. Took some of your mother's trinkets, luckily most of her valuables are still in town — but snatched my purse, the scoundrels. It would have been a different story had I had my pistol with me. I warrant you, I won't be travelling again without it.'

'Come Felix,' Lady Horton said. 'I am persuaded things could have been so very much worse. Had you had your pistol, we might have been shot. There were two of them, you know, and they were big burly fellows,' she added to Sophie.

Lord Horton deposited his many-caped greatcoat with the footman and strode off in the direction of his study and very probably the whisky decanter. A glass of ratafia and biscuits were sent for and Sophie drew her mama into the small sitting room where she had been doing her embroidery.

'Now we may be comfortable together and you can tell me all about it,' said Sophie as Lady Horton sank onto the settle with a sigh of relief.

'There is not so very much to tell,' she said eventually. 'We had been warned at our last coaching stop that the Highwaymen had been active again through Epping, but we did not expect it in broad daylight and certainly not so close to Enfield.'

'Was it not exciting?'

Lady Horton smiled. 'It was an

excitement I could well have spared myself, Sophie. Your stepfather was incensed by the audacity of the robbers, and I was very afraid for what he might do to put us all at risk. Old Barlow, our driver, is not a young man, you know, and the new footman we had with us is so very inexperienced. However, all is well. Just a few trinkets taken and your stepfather's purse in which he carried some winnings from the tables — and was none too willing to give up I can assure you.'

A tray bearing ratafia and biscuits was deposited on a small sewing table next to Sophie.

'Here Mama, some refreshment.' Sophie poured the sweet drink into a glass and passed it to her mother who, despite dismissing the adventure as being a trifling inconvenience, was looking paler than her usual self. 'Did you say there were two ruffians?'

Lady Horton nodded. 'Yes, two.'

'And did they speak?'

'Only a few rough words. 'Begging

your pardon yer Lordship, we'll be partaking of yer geegaws.' Something similar to that,' quoted Lady Horton in a deep rasping voice.

Sophie giggled. 'Mama, that was excessively clever.' She clapped her hands. 'You must certainly tell Tom about this, he'll find it a great piece of entertainment.'

'I'm sure he will,' Lady Horton said dryly. 'But Sophie, although I do not make a great to do about this, I beg you will take it seriously and not put yourself at risk. Stay close to home till we know these villains are no longer plaguing the Epping roads.'

'Tom has already warned me of this. I have only taken a few rides, keeping to our own bridle ways,' Sophie reassured her.

'Tom was right to do so, and you a good girl to obey him.' Lady Horton sighed heavily and took a sip from her glass.

'Don't look so sad, Mama,' urged Sophie. 'It was only a few trinkets, you said so yourself.'

'It's not for my trinkets I sigh. It's for my own folly. I was carrying the sapphire necklace. Luckily it was packed in the secret compartment of the trunk and another carriage was not far behind us, so the robbers could not tarry . . . ' Her shoulders slumped. 'I have been a very foolish woman since your papa died.'

Sophie put her arms round her mother. 'Never say so. You are unharmed, and that's the main thing. A necklace is worth absolutely nothing compared to your safety.'

Lady Isobel gave Sophie a sad smile. 'I wasn't speaking of the necklace so much as the fact of my marrying again. My love, I have made a sad business of things. I rushed into this marriage, longing for a strong arm to support me in bringing up two spirited children, but it seems as though it is you and Tom who support me in my marriage to a weak and foolish man . . . '

She put a shaky hand to her brow.

'And now I am worrying you too, with my troubles. Sometimes, truly, I feel I am not worthy to be a mother.'

'Now you're being nonsensical,' Sophie said. 'It's the shock, very likely. Tom has spoken a little to me about the way that we are situated, and Mama, pray don't worry on my behalf for a fine marriage. So long as I do not actively dislike the person concerned, I would far rather make a modest marriage and perhaps settle down near Ellington so I should be always very near to you.'

Lady Horton looked at Sophie with a light of understanding in her eyes. 'I must confess I had hoped that your feelings might lead you to settle close to home, but we have plenty of time to consider. You are only eighteen and everything that a good daughter should be, Sophie.' Her blue eyes, that so nearly matched the sapphires of the dowry necklace, suddenly twinkled. 'Well, so it seems today, at all events. Thank you, my love . . . And now I shall go to my room and rest a little after my journey.'

After kissing her daughter once more on the cheek, Lady Horton left the room. Sophie's face burned as she thought of how she had secretly met with Julian, three times now, and listened to poetry that was so very romantic — even if not precisely dedicated to her. She turned back to her embroidery, in an effort to indeed be the dutiful daughter her mother thought her to be.

3

The following afternoon was sunny and calm. After a morning of consultation with Tom and Lady Horton as to various estate duties that should be performed, Sophie was at last free to take her afternoon ride.

She hurried towards the stables, pleased that she had managed to avoid any questioning from Tom as to where she was going. On seeing her, Robin, the head groom who had been with the family since Sophie's babyhood, went directly to saddle up Regency Buck, Lizzie's horse that, as Harry had predicted, suited Sophie very well.

'Hello Buckie,' Sophie said producing a carrot from her pocket. 'All eagerness for a ride, I trust?'

But before the groom could throw her into the saddle there was a clatter on the cobblestones and Harry turned in at the stable yard. 'Good afternoon, Sophie,' he said grinning as he pulled his horse up alongside her. 'How is Regency Buck behaving?'

'Well enough, aren't you Buckie Boy?' Sophie answered with a smile. 'I try to exercise him every day, and he has shown nothing but good manners. I'm indebted to Lizzie for allowing me to ride him. Tom is always so patronising about my riding, and allows me only Apple Pie, when I am quite capable of the more spirited mounts. Well, Firefly at least.'

'Lizzie will be delighted at your exercising Regency Buck, as am I, for I promised her I would keep him fit. So you are doing us both a good turn. I don't know what she'd say to your calling him 'Buckie Boy' though.'

Harry looked across at her, staring rather longer than usual at her upturned face. His strong hands gently controlled his horse's reins, as halfway to dismounting, he seemed to change his mind and remained in the saddle. 'I have a capital notion. Tom was not expecting me today. If I were to ride with you, I could report back to Tom on how well you manage Lizzie's horse and then maybe he will be better-humoured towards your riding Firefly. What do you say?'

Sophie was uncomfortably aware that her face was colouring and that she was strangely loath to look Harry square in the eyes, while she fumbled for an excuse in order to continue unaccompanied and keep her tryst with Julian. To cover her confusion she lifted her skirts, placed one foot in the stirrup and waited for the groom to help her into the saddle.

'Really Harry, it's exceedingly good of you to offer, but I don't in the least mind riding alone, and I'm sure Tom will be pleased to see you . . . There's an incident happened just yesterday that I'm persuaded he will enjoy sharing with you.'

The light disappeared from Harry's eyes. 'I see,' he said looking at her narrowly. 'Well, of course if you are of a mind to ride alone, I shan't intrude. But we have enjoyed many an outing together in the past, I'm sure there could be no objection to us riding together for a short while. I am convinced a groom could be spared to accompany us if you wished.'

Sophie was feeling even worse now. 'Harry, you are too good, but I must decline; not for want of a groom, either. I am persuaded that if you had not come over to see Tom he would have come over to you, for I know he wishes to see you. And if you don't go directly to see him I'm sure I will spill the story — and that he would never forgive.'

At last he dismounted and Sophie heaved a sigh of relief.

'Well, I can't think what this news can be that is of such import.' Harry's usually good-natured face was wearing a frown as, with a word of thanks, he passed his horse's reins to the groom.

Sophie smiled, bid him goodbye and urged Regency Buck to walk briskly from the stables, without looking back to see the expression of puzzlement in Harry's eyes.

It was more than strange, she thought, as she allowed herself a gentle trot along the bridle path, that she should suddenly feel so very uncomfortable with Harry, whom she had known all of her life and was like a brother to her. Why suddenly should she feel so very ill at ease in deceiving him, whilst misleading both him and Tom in the past over all manner of trivial things had almost been a matter of sport?

Resolutely, Sophie decided to put all thoughts of Harry out of her mind. It was Julian of whom she should be thinking. When she reached the old barn and saw Julian's horse tethered within, her heart started beating in the erratic fashion she had come to expect at the out set of these deliciously secret, meetings.

'Julian,' she called as she dismounted — just slightly disappointed that he hadn't been looking out for her arrival.

Julian stood with his back to her, apparently so lost in his own private reverie that he had failed to hear her approach. He turned his head fractionally, so she was more able to admire his godlike profile.

'Ah, Sophie,' he said sadly. 'You are as balm to my soul.'

'Am I?' Sophie enquired, her heart fluttering quite uncontrollably under her riding habit. 'I'm sorry if I'm a little late. I met Harry in the stables and he wanted to ride with me, to make sure I was handling his sister's horse correctly, I expect, for I can think of no other reason why he should do so. At all events I managed to persuade him otherwise.'

'Harry?' Julian frowned.

'Yes, Harry Crighton. You surely must remember Harry. He was the only one of all the children hereabouts who managed to climb to the top of the old village oak on the green. He fell and broke his wrist on the way down again . . . Do you not recall?'

A nerve twitched in Julian's pale cheek. 'Of course. Harry . . . A friend of your brother Tom, as I remember.'

'That's right,' Sophie encouraged. It suddenly occurred to her that sometimes, speaking to Julian was rather like having a conversation with a not very bright five-year-old. 'The pair of them were certainly the scourge of the neighbourhood.'

'Indeed,' agreed Julian without the vestige of a smile.

'Anyway, how are you, Julian?' Sophie asked, already sensing that he was in ill humour.

Julian gave a languid sigh. 'I am afraid I am quite dispirited again. While you are all that is good and true, Sophie, and it relieves me to be able to share my confidences with you, alas, I fear that on occasion my sensitivity overcomes me and I find myself back in the doldrums again.'

Having been born with a cheerful nature herself, Sophie found it difficult to understand the sensitivities with which Julian seemed so often to be plagued. 'Perhaps we should take a brisk ride,' she suggested. 'It would lift your humour and if we are seen, no one would think it strange that as we chanced upon each other, we continue our way together. After all we were childhood friends, were we not?'

'Childhood seems a long time past,' mourned Julian.

'Not so long, surely? You were very good to me, Julian, when I was struggling with my watercolours. I remember your saying that my skies had a certain bruised quality.'

'I did?' Julian queried, clearly amazed. 'That was good. I was good with words even then.'

There seemed no answer to this and as it became obvious that Julian was in no hurry to remount his horse, Sophie cast around for some other topic of conversation.

'Oh Julian, how could I have forgotten? You recall you asked me for a lock of my hair as a keepsake, a token of our friendship? Well, see I have cut you a piece . . . I took it from behind my ear, because it's curlier there and a lock of hair looks so much more attractive if it has a curl to it, don't you agree? And then I found this old locket in my trinket box, so this is where I have put it. Then, when you are feeling low, you can remember me as your childhood friend who doesn't like to think of you in poor spirits.'

'Ah, Sophie, you are so very sweet,' Julian said, taking from her the glass locket that enclosed the red-gold hair. 'I shall wear it next to my heart.' So saying, he slid it into his waistcoat pocket.

Sophie took a gulp of air, and a step closer, and waited to see if she would be kissed. She knew she should probably be a little concerned as to whether or not she would be ravished, but some instinct told her that in spite of Tom's veiled insinuations Julian was not really the ravishing type.

After standing in close proximity to him for a matter of thirty seconds during which time Julian made no move to look deep into her eyes or to wrap his arms around her and hold her in an impassioned embrace, Sophie turned away. 'I can't stay too long,' she said rather more coldly. 'Someone might miss me and become concerned because of the Highwaymen.'

If she had been seeking to engage his attention, this approach certainly proved successful.

'Highwaymen?' Julian repeated in a voice full of alarm.

At last, she had his undivided scrutiny, and was surprised to notice very real fear in the violet depths of his eyes. 'Oh, it was quite some miles from here,' she said hastily. 'Nearer to Enfield, so Mama said. She was journeying back from London with Lord Horton yesterday. No one was hurt and only a few trinkets and my stepfather's fob watch and purse were taken ... We were a trifle shocked because there are so few Highway robberies now, especially in daylight.'

'Exactly so.' Sophie was sure she could hear a tremble in Julian's voice. 'I'm sure there is no need to fear, Sophie.'

Indignantly Sophie opened her mouth to retort that she was excited, not frightened, because — surely everyone knew — Highwaymen were rarely violent. Indeed they very often flirted with their victims, and she had a very great fancy to be flirted with by a Highwayman. Just in time, though, she remembered that this was Julian to whom she was speaking, not Harry, whom it was perfectly acceptable to tease. Julian, with his multitude of sensitivities, would find these comments sadly lacking in decorum and think the less of her because of it.

'Have you ever been robbed, Julian?' Sophie asked instead.

'Only of my heart, dear Sophie, by a lady who failed to appreciate the very depths of my feelings for her.'

'Oh,' Sophie said, the novelty of sharing Julian's finer feelings of unrequited love, was now beginning to pall. 'You're speaking of Adele again, are you not? She was, after all, a married lady. Did you not realise, it was bound to end badly?'

The look Julian shot her was wounded in the extreme, and Sophie was immediately contrite. She put a tentative hand on his arm. 'I didn't mean to sound harsh, merely to say that there are many good things to be appreciated in life. You are by far too young to consider your life over because of a love that went wrong. Only consider: we have the summer ahead of us with entertainments, picnics and races. Just think what marvellous times we could have together with Tom and Harry and Lizzie, when she returns from her visit. Only of course Lizzie will want Buckie Boy back then, so I'll be left with poor Apple Pie again.'

Julian gave a barely disguised shudder. 'Apple Pie? Buckie Boy? Lizzie and

Harry? I can scarce contain myself.'

For a long moment, Sophie contemplated her romantic hero and found herself wishing that his temperament was as flawless as his outer appearance. Julian was all that was beautiful, to be sure. From his carefully tousled locks to the tips of his highly polished Hessian boots, he appeared every inch the hero. Why, then, did she feel the stirrings of unease?

'I think I should perhaps go,' she said. 'Mama is newly back from town and might miss me.' She waited, half hoping that, in the light of the Highwaymen story, Julian would volunteer to escort her to the boundaries of Ellington Park. Julian however, after clasping her hand and declaring her to be his only true friend, showed no signs of helping her onto the back of Regency Buck, merely holding the horse's head in a way that could almost be described as ineffectual.

Lost in contemplation as to just how long it was to be expected for someone of great sensibilities to get over unrequited love, Sophie trotted away from the barn. She was so lost in this reflection that she hardly noticed the approach of a lone rider until he was almost upon her.

'Well, Sophie,' Harry said. 'You enjoyed your ride, I trust?'

Colouring, for no good reason that she could think of, Sophie sat a little straighter in the saddle and looked Harry in the eye. 'Indeed I did. It was quite — quite . . . exhilarating.'

'Hmm,' Harry answered. 'I understand you have been asked not to leave Ellington land, until we are sure there are no more Highwaymen in the area?'

Sophie shrugged.

'Maybe that's why you were so anxious that I shouldn't accompany you on your ride?'

'Maybe,' Sophie agreed.

'Don't worry, your secret is safe with me.'

'What secret?' Sophie asked in alarm.

Harry narrowed his eyes. 'Why, that I

have just met you outside the boundaries, of course. I shan't say anything you needn't think I shall, once I have escorted you back safely. But I would ask you, Sophie, to respect Lady Horton's wishes. We know nothing about these Highwaymen and what new threat they may be bringing to our patch of country.'

Sophie breathed with relief. For a moment, she had thought Harry had seen her come from the barn. She gave him a dazzling smile. 'If it pleases you, Harry, you may ride with me a way, but even Tom thinks it fiddlesticks to suppose we are in any danger here, when we are so far from the main thoroughfare.'

Harry's horse responded in answer to the firm pressure from his thighs and turned about, so they rode alongside one another. Sophie stared for a moment at the leg muscles making themselves visible through the material of his riding breeches. Harry was a fine figure of a man, she conceded. His clothes might not be quite so well cut or made of the very latest in exquisite material, as those of Julian. His physique was certainly not so elegant as the willowy frame that was Julian's — but for all that, Harry had an easy style and manner, and a confident forthright approach which Sophie wondered why she'd never observed before.

'Why does Julian find you and Tom so disagreeable?'

'Eh? Where did that come from?' Harry said looking around as though someone else had spoken. 'Why should you suddenly think of Julian and whether or not we are bosom pals? We are not, of course.'

'I was merely wondering,' Sophie mumbled, very aware that she had nearly given away her trysts with Julian. 'You hardly disguise the fact that you don't like him.'

'Oh. Well, I wouldn't say we are sworn enemies. But we had little in common as children, and even less now we've grown older.'

'There must have been something though, for you both to be so set against him. Is it to do with the trouble he has recently been in?'

Harry, who had been riding a little ahead, reined in his horse until they were level. 'What have you been hearing? I suppose some house maid has been gossiping? . . . You surely haven't seen Julian, have you?'

'Of course not,' lied Sophie, wishing she could cross her fingers. 'Tom said Julian's disgrace was a petticoat matter.'

With a poker face and a straight back, Harry resumed his riding. 'Well, Tom says more than is seemly . . . but you would be well warned, Sophie, to guard your reputation. Julian can do you harm by association alone. He has played fast and loose with too many ladies' affections. Yes, and the last, a mere chit barely out of the schoolroom.'

'Did he ravish her?' Sophie asked with unladylike interest. 'And I had heard she was a married lady.'

'I can't perceive how it comes to pass

that I'm having this highly inappropriate conversation with you,' Harry said in a voice packed full of amused disbelief.

'Well, did he? Ravish her, I mean,' Sophie asked again, highly curious as to whether she'd been totally mistaken in believing Julian had no real desire to ravish anyone.

'I don't know, Sophie, and if I did I wouldn't tell you. Tom would never forgive me. Not the sort of thing to discuss with sisters of my friend.'

'Only one sister, and at any event, I don't care.'

'You'd care well enough if your reputation were to be in ruins from being seen with someone who is fast becoming known as a rake,' Harry said, the amusement gone from his voice.

Sophie laughed. 'Well, Harry, I never thought you'd turn the prosy old aunt on me. And you're surely hoaxing! I can't believe Julian to be a rake!'

Harry's face was flushed and angry and his eyes glittered dangerously. 'It doesn't matter what you believe. It's what other people, people of consequence, believe that sets the tone! He has caused more than one scandal so have a care, Sophie; any lady seen with him at present could be severely compromised, for a season at least.'

The laughter died on her lips. She hadn't meant to make Harry so angry. He'd never been angry with her before. Not like this. She opened her mouth to tell him she was sorry.

'You are being unjust to Julian, and a stuffed shirt into the bargain,' she found herself saying instead. 'I would have thought you to extend the hand of friendship in Julian's hour of need. Not believe everything that's bad before you've had counsel with him.' Her colour was heightened in tune with her indignation. 'We're on Ellington land now, so I'll thank you for your escort. I don't know why you're being so hateful but I'd rather ride alone for the rest of the way.'

For a long moment she looked into

Harry's normally twinkling eyes. There was no smile in sight.

'As you please, Sophie.'

He turned his horse and rode off at a canter.

4

It was three days later. Three days in which Sophie had dutifully paid morning calls to various tenants on the estate in the company of Lady Horton, respectfully tried to understand some of the household expenditure with Mrs Cope, the housekeeper at Ellington Park and, in her spare time, tried and failed, to catch up with her embroidery.

Of course Julian was never far from her thoughts. The May weather had continued to be more like April with its changeability and Sophie had only once been able to ride out alone to the old barn. There, she had left a hastily written note, explaining that her time was presently curtailed, and had secreted it in their usual hiding place under a piece of rock near the old water trough.

Poor, tortured, misunderstood Julian. How dare Harry be so dismissive of the anguish he was going through? Sophie accidentally stabbed herself with her sewing needle, and that was Harry's fault too. It seemed she just had to think about him and unpleasant things happened. There was no cause for him to be so undoubtedly high-handed with her. It was beyond all that was reasonable for him to have been so cold, so suddenly unforgiving. Where had the old fun-loving Harry gone? The Harry she could say anything to — *did* say anything to? The Harry she was comfortable with.

She looked up without any real interest as Tom strolled into the room. 'Raining again,' he said conversationally. Then he sprawled onto a low chair and dealt himself some cards. Sophie continued with the now literally blood-red poppy she was embroidering. Tom tutted and tapped his teeth with his cards, then wondered several times aloud, why Harry had not ridden over to pay his respects.

'Three days — it has only been three days, Tom. I am sure we can manage for three days without his company,' Sophie said crossly and with barely concealed impatience.

After pausing on the threshhold in order to listen to this conversation, Lady Isabel Horton, with a rustle of cambric, swept into the small withdrawing room. 'Well tomorrow, Tom, you and Sophie and I will pay a call on the Reverend Crighton and Harry, and also on Lord and Lady Stafford-Smythe. They are both in the same direction and I believe there's been some silliness on account of Julian kicking up a dust in town. It's high time I made a morning call to prevent them being ostracised by the neighbourhood. Really, it's too tiresome, Lady Stafford has always so many ailments to discuss and I fear her son is not much better, but we must see if we can lift their melancholy — must we not? No doubt that ninny Julian has learned his lesson by now and has been in disgrace long enough.'

'That's all very well, Mama,' Tom said hotly. 'It would be a very different kettle of fish, I'll warrant, if I had been sent home in disgrace.'

Lady Isobel gave Tom a speaking look. 'My dear Tom, I credit you with a deal more sense than Julian's ever had. His problem is he has a melancholy disposition and a loose tongue, quite apart from a passion for the stage.'

'A passion for the stage?' Sophie, who was only just recovering from hearing her mother describe her hero as a ninny, repeated.

'Melodrama, my love,' her mother explained shortly. 'Well, we can all do foolish things on occasion. So long as no one is irrevocably damaged, least said, soonest mended is my opinion.'

'Oh, I do so agree with you Mama,' Sophie said, feeling brighter with every moment.

★ ★ ★

However when the next morning dawned and the carriage was brought round to the main entrance, Sophie found she was feeling more than a little nervous. It was the thought of seeing, not Julian with all his brooding neurosis, but Harry, whom, she now knew, could put her out of countenance at a glance.

At Tom's insistence he was to accompany their carriage, riding Firefly postilion. 'It's not that I'm feeling in the least nervous,' Lady Horton explained to Sophie. 'Those Highwaymen are long gone. But I've discovered that sometimes, my love, it yields dividends to make a man feel beholden to you for allowing him to do exactly what he planned in the first place. Particularly if it has the appearance of great sacrifice, and yet fits with one's own plans.'

Briefly, Sophie wondered why it was that Lady Horton was considered to be a beautiful woman, but with no pretensions to any great intelligence, when her daughter knew her to be wise above the commonplace.

'I shall keep a good lookout, Mama, you may depend upon it,' Tom called from his place next to the leader horse.

'Thank you, Tom. As you insist — we can do nothing but be very much obliged,' replied Lady Horton with a serene smile.

Although the rectory was less than a quarter of the hour's canter from Ellington Park across country, by carriage on the main highway it took more than twice that time. During the journey, Sophie spent several heartfelt minutes in trying to persuade Lady Horton to prevail upon Tom to allow her to ride Firefly. 'Or how will I ever hope to improve, Mama, if I'm to be forever compelled to ride Apple Pie? Only look how well Firefly behaves with Tom.'

'What does Harry think?' her mother asked, not without a little mischief.

'What has Harry to do with it?'

'Well, he is the best horseman and judge of horseflesh for miles.' Her eyes twinkled. 'I beg you do not betray this confidence to your brother, however, Sophie.'

'Well, H-Harry — ' To her annoyance Sophie found she stumbled a little over the name. 'He judged me well enough to exercise Regency Buck for Lizzie while she's away. But she will be back very soon, and although I do love Apple Pie, I would dearly love to progress to Firefly. Tom only rides him when completing some tame chore, as today.'

Lady Horton smiled. 'I'll see what I can do, my love.'

With that, Sophie had to be content as Lady Horton went on to enquire how Sophie had fared with Mrs Cope that morning.

'Well, I must confess, Mama, to not precisely having enjoyed it, but I do understand your point about knowing how a great house must be run.'

'My love,' Lady Horton replied lightly, 'there's many a time I have wished I had taken more time when your father was alive, to familiarise myself both with the running of the Estate and with household expenditure. Tom is doing well with Estate management so it is only right and fair that you take your part too. And where Mrs Cope does an excellent job here at Ellington Park, if it were to come to pass that you marry a man in more straitened circumstances than ourselves, the ability to balance the household accounts would stand you in very good stead.'

Lady Isobel then went on to discuss the invitation received that morning for their attendance at a dinner for the local gentry, to be held by a Count and Countess of Frimlington, who had taken a house in the area for the summer. The remainder of the journey was spent in contemplation of which gowns would be suitable for the occasion. Lady Horton deciding on a blue brocade over satin gown, which had cost her an extortionate amount of money, for herself, and a high-waisted, tiny puffed sleeved cream muslin over cream silk for Sophie, as she was not yet officially 'out'.

'Wear your pearls, my love, they flatter your skin; also the blue and cream silk shawl because it brings out the colour of your eyes. My eyes used to be the same blue, you know; your Papa was used to compare them to the sapphire necklace. Quite a charming compliment, was it not?'

'Will you wear the necklace?' Sophie asked.

'Well, I have a notion to, I must confess. There seems little point in having the sapphires if they are always to remain locked up, unseen.'

On arrival at the rectory, Lady Horton was invited to partake in a dish of tea, and Sophie to take a stroll round the gardens which were looking particularly lovely after the recent showers followed by sunshine. Tom, after enquiring the date set for Lizzie's return, rode on to look for Harry. The rector thought he had gone in the direction of Home Farm.

Sophie wandered through the rambling area that was the rector's garden and finished her preamble to sit on an old bench in the herb garden. It was peaceful here, with the bees buzzing around lavender bushes that were not quite in flower, and where two doves coyly followed each other along the brick paths towards a shallow sunken pool. Her mother, she knew, would spend considerable time with the rector in the discussion of various parishioners on the estate who were undergoing hardship of any kind, and what could be done to alleviate their problems.

There was a soft footfall. A serious-faced Harry came towards her.

Sophie remembered her mother's wise words and smiled accordingly. 'Harry, I cannot like this — this no longer being your friend. Why do you no longer smile at me?'

Harry came closer and bared his teeth, which although not perfectly straight were very white and shiny, in a travesty of a smile.

'A proper smile.'

'Oh so, it's a proper smile you require from your 'hateful' friend now.'

Sophie turned her head towards him in surprise that he should remember her words so accurately. 'That was my temper . . . and I'm sorry for it. I hope we will find no further need to mention it. Now, tell me what did you think of the robbery poor Mama and Lord Horton were subjected to? Did Mama give her impression of the Highway-man?'

Harry gave a thin-lipped smile. 'No indeed, but your brother gave an impression of her impression and it was very droll. But seriously, Sophie, you should have a care. Stay on Ellington land if you must ride alone.'

'What's happened to you, Harry?' Sophie asked, endeavouring to keep her tone light. You used to be fun-loving; now it seems you are all that is worthy and boring.'

'Perhaps I always was — boring and worthy — and it has taken you until now to realise it.'

'Never say so, Harry, for you know it isn't true. I'm sorry our last meeting went so poorly. I felt you to be overbearing in the same way as Tom is used to being. One brother is more than enough to contend with. He too gives me orders and hints at half-truths about things not deemed seemly to discuss with a lady. And whilst I appreciate your delicacy of mind, I would inform you that even Mama has a fair understanding of Julian's nature and does not regard his latest escapade to carry too much import.'

An exasperated sigh escaped Harry's lips. 'Well Sophie, maybe that's because even your mother does not always understand the truth of the matter. Men like Julian, who act the part of misunderstood souls, seem to be able to hoax even the most sensible of females. They just go through life trading on their good looks, status and charm. Julian's previous affair, with a married woman, was indiscreet to say the least, but this last dalliance was beyond all that is decent.'

'Pray continue, tell me more,' Sophie encouraged Harry very quietly.

Harry sighed. 'Very well; I see that you are beyond all patience to know. Julian met a beautiful, but naive young heiress who was hardly out of the schoolroom. He flirted with her, arranged to meet her alone and took her to the Vauxhall Gardens — not the sort of place to take a young unchaperoned lady, as you well know. She surely should have known she was putting her reputation at risk.

'While it's true Julian probably acted out of a selfish disregard for the consequences of his actions, than intent to compromise her, the result is the same. No wonder he is in disgrace — he deserves to be, it could have caused a huge scandal.'

'I see,' said Sophie who had struggled hard not to say 'fudge' or 'fiddlesticks' at certain points in his narrative. 'Well, you make it sound all that is serious, but . . . '

'Julian's a fool,' interrupted Harry. 'But then, he always was. The lady involved should have known better, been better cared for by her friends and family . . . You, I am persuaded would have had more sense. I am telling you this, Sophie, to impress upon you that young men of Julian's ilk are always best avoided.'

Sophie bit back the retort that she thought him to be a po-faced cabbage head, which was something that just a few short weeks ago she would not have hesitated to voice. No; this new mealy-mouthed Harry had to be treated with caution if she didn't want to be out of sorts with him all over again.

'Well,' Sophie said in what she hoped was an agreeable tone, 'There are no Vauxhall Gardens here, so that particular temptation is unlikely to be thrown in my path. We are in the country, Harry; the town is a different matter. I think my mother is right, we can't make life uncomfortable for our neighbours because of an incident that happened in town. It's for this reason that we are on our way this very morning to pay a call on the Stafford-Smythes. I am persuaded it won't be so very terrible.'

For a moment their gazes locked and a certain frisson of something intangible sizzled in the air between them. Then Harry looked away. 'As you please, Sophie. And now I must take my leave of you. Your brother awaits.'

Sophie stared after Harry's lithe but well-built figure in dismay. Where, oh, where had the old Harry gone? Where the comradeship and the easy banter? He had stood before her like a wooden soldier, as though he could barely endure to be in her company. There had been no light of even liking in his eyes, and his twinkle had not once made an appearance.

A hot teardrop landed on the back of her glove. Angrily, she brushed it away.

It was a beautiful morning and she was on her way in the company of her mother, who knew everything that was right and proper, to pay a morning call at the home of her hero, Julian.

5

But in the event, the visit to the Stafford-Smythe's ancestral home of Clayborough Manor proved to be dull in the extreme.

It was a full half hour after their arrival that a sullen-faced Julian put in an appearance. As always, the mere sight of him was enough to make Sophie feel awe-struck and breathless but, despite her best endeavours to engage him in idle conversation, his mood did not incline to lighten.

'Did you retrieve my note?' whispered Sophie, whilst Lady Horton and Lady Stafford-Smythe were deep in a discussion regarding remedies for inflammation of the lungs. With a slight nod of the head Julian indicated that he had.

'Will you meet me again soon, Sophie?' he murmured back. 'It is so devilish flat here at the moment, and our little interludes have a way of lifting my spirits somewhat.'

'I will try for tomorrow afternoon,' replied Sophie, trying not to conjecture that she was being considered as no more than a dose of smelling salts. 'For I must exercise Lizzie's horse again before she comes home. It would be better advised, though, Julian, if we were to meet as though by accident then continue our ride together,' she added as an afterthought because, in spite of herself, she was beginning to feel a little uncomfortable about their clandestine meetings. 'I'm sure that no one could object to that.'

'Tomorrow then, near the barn,' Julian promised.

Shortly after that, the carriage and horses were walked back to the imposing front entrance and Lady Isobel and Sophie made their farewells.

'Our visit was timely, I perceive,' remarked Lady Isobel. 'They also, have received an invitation to the dinner at

Clayborough Manor to be held by Count and Countess Frimlington.'

'Really? So Julian might be there?'

'Oh I should imagine so. Time to eat humble pie and be all that is obliging, as no doubt his parents have made him aware.'

'Hmm,' Sophie reconsidered the cream silk underdress, wondering if maybe the pale blue would be more flattering.

Lady Isobel settled herself more comfortably on her seat in the carriage. 'Julian must be quite the most handsome young man it has been my good fortune to clap eyes on.'

'Yes indeed. That is . . . Well, I'll own his eyes are bright and quite above the commonplace.'

'Eyelashes any girl would envy, and such white, soft skin too,' continued Lady Isobel watching her daughter from under half-closed lids.

'And his hair so black . . . '

'Black as a raven's wing,' agreed Lady Isobel.

The carriage picked up speed and both ladies swayed from side to side with the motion.

'Of course his chin is just a little weak,' mused Lady Isobel almost to herself. 'And his mouth on occasion, can appear quite sullen.'

Sophie said nothing, thinking unbidden of Harry's firm, square jaw and wide, good-humoured mouth, which, she surprised herself by recalling, produced a dimple on his left cheek whenever he laughed. Strange that she should have noticed unaware.

'But overall,' concluded Lady Isobel, 'I would have to agree he is every inch the desirable dandy.'

'He's not a dandy, Mama!' Sophie said, a little too heatedly.

Almost imperceptibly, Lady Isobel's eyebrows rose. 'No ... No, my love, perhaps not precisely a dandy. But he has a certain studied carelessness about him that is the very epitome of arrogant, rebellious youth ... He would make a splendid subject for a portrait.'

'Oh yes, he would,' agreed Sophie with glowing eyes.

'There would be room for no one else in the frame, naturally,' commented Lady Isobel after another few moments during which both ladies listened to the sound of the carriage wheels. Then, after another timely pause: 'It was good of Harry to bring Lizzie's horse over for you to ride. I expect he thought there would be more than one occasion to accompany you himself.'

Sophie bit her lip. 'Sometimes, Mama . . . '

'Yes, my love?'

'Sometimes, I can't help but fear that Harry is slowly turning into a very dull dog.'

Lady Isobel gave a faint smile. 'We all have to grow up at some point Sophie . . . Now then, we shall have tea when we arrive home. Then I shall see your stepfather who plans, the day after our dinner with the Count and Countess, to travel to Ireland to attend to his estates. I fear they have been sorely neglected of late.' She paused significantly. 'He, too, is a handsome man, Sophie . . . Think on it.'

★   ★   ★

The remainder of the day passed uneventfully for Sophie, terminating in a dinner with only Lord and Lady Horton for company. Later, after the two ladies had left Lord Horton to his port, Sophie discovered that Tom and Harry had been prevailed upon by both the Rector and Lady Isobel to include Julian into joining a card game set up by friends in the nearest town. They had all, presumably, dined there.

'I can't like your brother playing the tables regularly, but a local game of cards is no large experience — I'm persuaded no harm can come of it.'

'No indeed,' Sophie said, wondering that her mother should so suddenly be sharing her confidence in so many matters.

'Of course Lord Horton will not be

joining them. It is too tame an event for his participation so I did not mention it to him, Sophie — and I pray that you do not.'

'Absolutely not,' agreed Sophie again.

'I think that in Ireland he will be monstrous busy with estate matters, I doubt he will have time for games of hazzard.'

Sophie bowed her head over her embroidery and made no comment.

* * *

The following afternoon, Sophie made her way to the stables and watched as Robin saddled Regency Buck. She felt in the pocket of her new dark green riding habit for a sugar lump and stroked the horse's nose as she fed it to him.

Robin enquired as to whether she might require a groom as escort.

'Thank you not, Robin. I'll just proceed on my usual route not too far outside our boundaries. I have Mama's permission to go alone.'

With Robin's help, she swung into the side saddle which part of her despised, but which she knew was all that was decorous, and started off at a brisk trot. Once she was out of sight of the house, however, she urged her mount into a canter and arrived at the barn flushed and breathless. There was no sign of Julian.

At first the disappointment felt sharp, then Sophie wondered whether something had befallen him, or whether he had been prevented from joining her at the appointed time and had managed to leave a note for her earlier.

She was just bending to replace the stone, which she was irritated to find had not been hiding a secret missive for her, when she heard a footfall.

'Oh, it's you,' she said. Then felt her face flush fiery red as she realised how very impolite she must sound.

'You're not overcome with joy to see me then, Sophie,' replied Harry, staring at the stone in her hand. 'I thought maybe you had trouble with Regency Buck and that was why you pulled in here.'

'No,' Sophie said, dropping the stone as though it was red hot and crossing her fingers behind her back. 'Regency Buck is very well behaved, and thank you, Harry, for caring enough to follow me. I merely had a stitch in my side and paused for breath. I have Mama's permission to ride this far unaccompanied — so you needn't be so disobliging as to lecture me.'

'That's the last thing I should think of,' Harry replied with a tight smile.

Sophie searched frantically for something to say. All commonplaces regarding the weather or Tom's whereabouts or the price of corn this year, completely deserted her. Harry seemed equally at a loss and stood rooted to the spot, his eyes searching her face.

'I understand you played cards last evening,' Sophie said at last, in some desperation.

'Yes.'

'With Tom and Julian?'

'Amongst others, yes.'

'And the evening was convivial?'

Harry stroked his square jaw and just for a moment Sophie glimpsed a devilish twinkle in his eyes. 'You'd best ask Tom about that.'

'Why, what happened?'

Harry laughed, and Sophie immediately felt better. He hadn't changed after all; the old Harry was still there waiting to be found.

'I deduce you won money from him,' she guessed.

'It's not my story to tell,' Harry said. 'Now have you finished your ride? Would you like my company or no?'

'Of course,' said Sophie. 'As long as you promise not to get top lofty with me or lecture me like some prosey old aunt.'

'I promise,' said Harry. 'Now let's see you put Regency Buck through his paces.'

Outside the barn where the horses were tethered alongside one another,

Harry put his hands together ready to receive her booted foot and toss her into the saddle. Although unaccountably loath so to do, Sophie put her hand on his shoulder to steady herself, as she had done so many times in the past. She felt the strength of him as he helped her, then sat staring into his hazel eyes feeling suddenly uncomfortably shy.

'Obliged to you, Harry,' she said shortly.

'Entirely at your service ma'am,' replied Harry grinning. 'No excessive showing off now, just a gentle, ladylike canter.'

'Fiddlesticks, Harry,' Sophie answered with a wicked smile. 'Go Buckie Boy! Go!' And in spite of the side-saddle she urged Regency Buck to a furious gallop.

* * *

By the time Sophie arrived home from her ride, she found she'd given no further thought to Julian's having failed to keep their tryst, or indeed to have left any note by way of explanation. Harry and she had chased together like children, through the woods, ducking the dangerously low, overhanging branches, splashing through streams and cantering through meadows, whose seeds were sleeping now, but in two months' time would be a sea of wild flowers. Sophie didn't know when she had enjoyed herself more. Once she was safely back inside the boundaries of Ellington Park, Harry took his leave of her.

'Thank you, Harry, I enjoyed the afternoon,' Sophie said, leaning forward to pat Regency Buck's neck in an attempt to disguise the fact that another strange paralysis of the tongue had overcome her.

'Your very obedient servant, Sophie,' replied Harry with a salute before he turned his horse and headed back towards the rectory.

As she reached her bed chamber, she caught herself singing under her breath and glancing in the mirror, saw that her cheeks were flushed, her eyes sparkling and how trim her figure appeared in her new green riding habit. If only Julian had kept their engagement today, she thought, he was sure not to have been able to resist her.

★ ★ ★

'Ah Tom — a little light in the pocket I understand, after your card game with Julian?'

It was breakfast time the next morning, and for some inexplicable reason Sophie was feeling happier than she had done for days.

Tom looked at his sister in bewilderment. 'I declare you to become more addle brained by the day,' he replied.

A selection of silver salvers were lined up on the heavy sideboard. Sophie lifted a cover and partook herself a generous helping of ham and eggs. 'Perhaps I don't have the right of it then. I met Harry yesterday and when I pressed him as to your evening's entertainment, he said you would bring me up to snuff . . . He seemed more than a little amused.'

Her only answer to that was the steady champing of Tom's jaws.

'Devilish fine fellow, Harry,' Tom said eventually. 'But he should learn to keep a closer tongue in his head.'

'So you did lose to Julian?'

Tom's expression became a little belligerent. 'That's where you're wrong. I took the blunt from Julian, as it happens. No satisfaction in it, mind. Like taking milk from a baby. He's such a prize nincompoop . . . It's not as though we played for high stakes at all. Only a friendly game — at Harry's insistence. Come to think of it, old Harry's been acting a shade touched in the upper storey lately. Kept talking about extending the hand of friendship to a man down on his luck. Took me a while to figure out he was referring to that nincompoop Julian. Julian of all people!' Shaking his head at the senselessness of it all, Tom went back to concentrating on wiping his plate with a hunk of bread.

'He's not a nincompoop!'

'No, well, you wouldn't think so. You ain't much better yourself. No need to get on your high ropes about it, though. And Julian might not be a nincompoop, but he ain't a good loser. Accused me of cheating!'

Sophie paused with a forkful of ham halfway to her lips. 'Oh no, Tom, surely he wouldn't do that . . . ' Then after another moment, 'You *weren't* cheating, were you?'

Tom's face flushed with indignation. 'Call yourself my sister and you ask me that? Unquestionably, I wasn't cheating and so you should know! Devilish annoying, even so. And I know everyone knows Julian's a dashed queer cove and there's no accounting with what he'll come out with next. Even so, dashed nearly called him out. If it hadn't been for Harry, would have done too. Taught the fellow a lesson. Can't have a fellow calling me a cheat — cabbage head or not!'

Oh dear. Sophie finished her ham and eggs and called for more coffee. 'Julian probably didn't mean it to sound just exactly as it did,' she suggested eventually.

' "You sir, are a cheat,' was what he said exactly. I don't think the meaning could be any more transparent, do you? Harry's right, though. Julian's a bit caper-witted — stands to reason, probably all that poetry turned his mind. He's not worth bothering about, and I won't in future — no matter what Mama says.' Tom wiped his mouth with his napkin. 'Had the effrontery to suggest to us a further card evening at a friend's place near Enfield, to give him a chance to recoup his winnings. Can't perceive what a friend of Julian's could possibly be like — in fact it's hard to believe he actually has any friends! Couldn't believe my ears . . . Harry cried off for the both of us, saying we had a previous engagement.'

Poor Julian, Sophie thought sadly. It seemed he was now in everyone's bad graces.

Then she remembered that he had failed to keep his appointment with her, failed even to leave a message under the stone, and began to believe that perhaps Julian did have his weaknesses.

She needed a friend to share confidences with.

'I'm glad Lizzie's back tomorrow,' she said to Tom's back as he strode from the room. 'I should dearly love to see her and I must return Regency Buck to her of course.'

Tom turned in the doorway. 'I'll take him back to her if it pleases you,' he said. 'She seems to have been gone a long time, said so to Mama just yesterday. I've a mind to ride out with Lizzie myself soon. She's good in the saddle, not one for having the vapours at the first drop of rain. Yes, that's a capital notion!'

Shrugging, Sophie went back to the business of finishing her breakfast, thinking, nevertheless, how typically high-handed it was of Tom to assume that Lizzie would prefer to ride with him than his sister, and what an exceedingly disagreeable brother he was. However, her morning duties with Mrs Cope loomed.

Once luncheon was finished, Sophie changed into her green riding habit and slipped down to the stables, hoping that Tom hadn't already taken Regency Buck back to the rectory. If he hadn't, she would just exercise Lizzie's horse as she had promised, and should Julian happen to be near the barn, by coincidence, then surely there was nothing to stop her passing the time of day with him. It wasn't as though she had an appointment with him any longer, and she certainly felt it unbecoming in the extreme to leave messages for someone who deemed it unnecessary to answer them.

Nevertheless, this afternoon as she slowly circled the barn, keeping a sharp eye out for any approaching riders,

Sophie came to the conclusion that there was no reason for her to continue meeting Julian in this underhand manner. While it was no doubt all very romantic and exciting, at the outset anyway, she had to admit that lately, more particularly when Harry was in the vicinity, she had begun to feel uneasy about it.

Yes, the next time she saw Julian she would explain that as Mama had now paid a morning call to his home, it would be considered all that was seemly for him to return that morning call. From then on, they could bear each other company in a conventional manner that was surely more fitting to the both of them. Then she caught herself wondering whether she might find a morning call from Julian perhaps a little wearisome.

Her cheeks started burning at the disloyalty of the notion. This was Julian she was thinking about. Julian with his violet eyes, his coal-black locks and, she realised with a shock, his inability to laugh at himself. Just as she was about to turn again towards the barn, Sophie pulled Regency Buck up at speed, and pointed him instead back towards Ellington Park.

⋆ ⋆ ⋆

The normal hour for dining at Ellington Park was five o'clock. Sophie found herself ready a little early, so she thought to go to the library which was quite her favourite room at this time of day. It faced west, and the evening sun slanted through the large casement windows bathing the faded grandeur of the old carpets and the wall of books with their spines of tooled leather, in a pink-tinged evening light.

The door was ajar and Sophie paused on the threshold, pondering on the faint tapping she could hear from within. Silently, she took two paces into the room and saw Lord Horton, with his back to her, apparently intent on removing several books from the library shelves and tapping at the wood panelling behind them. Sophie's eyes grew round as the significance of this made itself felt.

She took two steps back out into the hallway and rattled the door knob loudly before re-entering the room. By this time, Lord Horton was replacing the books and looked over his shoulder with his normal charming smile.

'Ah, Sophie! You look so very pretty this evening. You have such a look of your mother about you. I declare it to be unfair to have two such beautiful women under the same roof.'

Sophie smiled in reply, then went on to exchange commonplaces about the weather, the freshness and charm of the Ellington woods in springtime, and an enquiry as to her stepfather's gout, from which he suffered from to time.

But in the back of her mind she was wondering how long it would be before he reached the E for Ellington section, which hid the secret compartment where the sapphire necklace was lodged.

6

Sophie sat hunched over the household account ledger. Not for the first time, she wondered why items were bought by the dozen or half dozen rather than in tens. Also why the columns of figures had to go on for a whole page instead of ending in a subtotal half way down, which would make tracing an error in arithmetic so much easier. On pointing this out to Mrs Cope however, she was met with a frosty silence followed by a sniff and a rejoinder that this was always the way it had been done and had given constant satisfaction in the past, to be sure.

Realising that she'd made a grave error of judgement in voicing her thoughts aloud, Sophie spent the next five minutes in praising Mrs Cope for her neat figure work and on her powers of mental arithmetic, which Sophie was sure she could in no way match. Slightly mollified, Mrs Cope left Sophie to finish the last column of figures alone, saying she would check it later.

'Lizzie's back!' Tom stood in the doorway grinning all over his face. 'A groom has just come from the rectory to lead Regency Buck back to her. Then it is suggested we take a ride together after luncheon. You too, of course, and I daresay Harry, if he has finished advising the farm tenants.'

'It seems you are more excited to see Lizzie than I,' Sophie commented with a raised eyebrow. 'But then you were strangely smug at breakfast, as though you were bursting to tell me about some hum or other.' She sighed and turned back to her books. 'I hope you realise that now I have to start afresh with this column of figures . . . Have you never thought, Tom, it would be so very much easier were we to buy things in tens instead of twelves? And also to have, for example, ten inches to a foot and maybe even ten pennies to a shilling?'

'Eh?' Tom said, looking completely baffled. 'Can't do that, Sophie. Ain't done. How would you describe a man of six foot tall? Couldn't do it, could you? Sort of nonsensical suggestion a female would come out with . . . At any event, be sure to be on time for luncheon so we may have a decent ride.'

He turned away whistling, then came back, as an afterthought struck him. 'Harry says you are good enough for Firefly.' He pursed his lips for a moment. 'I hope he may be right. You must go gently on his mouth, though, but be strong with your knees. I would wish you to borrow my breeches and ride him astride at first, but I daresay you won't care for that in company. Though it's only Lizzie, of course, and old Harry, and he wouldn't give a fig.'

Sophie fixed Tom with an icy stare. 'I'm surprised at you indeed, my so particular brother, that you suggest something so unseemly. You, who lecture me so freely on my lack of decorum. Now leave me in peace to finish my sums if you would like me to be punctual for luncheon.'

★　★　★

After luncheon however, as Sophie — albeit side-saddle — rode with Tom across to the rectory, she could not resist showing off a little. First she daintily walked Firefly, then gradually urged him into a trot and then to a very sedate canter. She had more sense than to progress to a full gallop, even though she felt Firefly to be an easier horse to manage than Regency Buck, who was used to Lizzie's rather more flamboyant style of horsemanship.

She could see Tom about to open his mouth and comment that she was becoming over-confident. 'Thank you so much, Tom, for allowing me to ride Firefly,' she said quickly. 'I must own that he is quite the most gentle of creatures. You have trained him beautifully, for I well remember when he first came to our stable, his manners were not so good.' *There, Mama*, she thought as Tom flushed modestly at such sisterly praise, *see how I have learned from you.*

But later, when they had joined up with Harry and Lizzie, who had ridden out to meet them, Sophie began to wish she hadn't been quite so agreeable to Tom. He seemed to be paying Lizzie so much attention that Sophie had hardly a moment to speak with her alone, and no chance at all for confidences of a girlish nature. Harry also appeared to be acting in a manner that could only be described as distant, and Sophie had to keep reminding herself that the last time they'd ridden together it had been with the easy comradeship which symbolised their lifelong friendship. But today, although he was all that was polite, his smile was cool and he kept his horse an aloof length away from Firefly.

Nevertheless, it was a beautiful spring day and Sophie was not one to let herself become blue-devilled for no very good reason other than that no one seemed to be taking much notice of her. Soon she was concentrating on putting Firefly through his paces and was presently rewarded by Lizzie stating that Regency Buck had been kept in good form, and going on to compliment Sophie on her improved riding abilities and excellent handling of Firefly.

Sophie flushed with pleasure. 'It was Harry who suggested I ride your horse in your absence, and I own I did very much enjoy it, but Firefly has always been the horse I most wanted to ride. He has such spirit, and is so very handsome, and I find I love him quite as much as I expected.'

'All right, Sophie,' said Tom clearly embarrassed. 'You don't have to prose on about it. He's only a horse.'

'Hello,' said Lizzie, straining her eyes against the sunlight. 'Who's this coming towards us? . . . Surely, it cannot be . . . It is! It's Julian.'

Sophie nearly fell off Firefly with shock, but collected herself in time and watched with amazement as Julian cantered, *cantered*, in their direction. He was cantering, which on its own was something Sophie had never seen him attempt before, and with a wild abandon for the safety of his person that was a far cry from his usual languid manner of transporting himself. Surely, something must be amiss.

After her astonishment, Sophie's first thought was that at last Julian would be able to feast his eyes on her new, green, form-hugging riding habit. But this thought was forced into the background by her concern that her hero surely must have taken leave of his senses, to risk his biscuit-coloured riding breeches and highly polished boots becoming badly spattered by the mud that spewed up all around him. In normal circumstances he would be horrified at the very notion.

All four of the party stood their mounts still as statues, as they watched the approach of this somewhat comical figure. Tom's mouth had dropped slightly open with amazement, Lizzie was looking equally surprised, and Harry — well, Harry had a sleepy-eyed amused expression on his face, which made him look a little more like the old Harry once more.

'Heavens, Julian,' Lizzie called as he drew within hailing distance. 'Is there a fire we fail to see?'

'No, there is not,' replied Julian when he had recovered his breath. 'I have come out, on the advice of my mother, merely for a breath of fresh air and in an effort to cast the terrible events of last eve from my mind.'

'Oh, Julian, what has befallen you?' asked Sophie regarding his careworn appearance in alarm.

'I underwent the most awful of experiences,' Julian went on as though Sophie had not spoken. 'I was returning from my card party at Enfield, when I was set upon by three ruffians.'

'Three?' Harry echoed, his eyebrows

rising in surprise.

'Yes, three,' said Julian firmly. 'Huge fellows they were. The ugliest customers you have ever encountered . . . They surrounded me. Demanded my valuables.'

'Well, I doubt you had much, unless your luck at cards changed from the usual,' said Tom, his eyes dancing with fun.

'The devils took my purse, which held quite some five guineas.'

'Five guineas?' repeated Harry again.

'Yes, and my fobs at my belt, not to mention a love token which was very close to my heart.'

'Oh dear,' Lizzie said. 'How monstrous.'

'Monstrous,' Sophie echoed faintly.

'Then they threatened me with my life! Almost knocked me from my horse, but of course I held my seat and cussed at them and warned them I would be after them.'

'That would be sure to terrify them,' Tom said, the suspicions of a smile hovering around his mouth.

'Of course you did,' said Harry at the same time. 'It's what any fellow would do.'

'Then they rode off towards London.'

'They must have been the very same gang who robbed Mama,' said Sophie, her eyes wide with excitement. 'Was it not very thrilling, Julian?'

The look Julian cast her indicated that he felt she was truly quite mad. 'Thrilling? To be threatened for my life? I might have been left for dead on the Highway.' Julian paled at the mere thought.

'But you weren't, were you?' Sophie said practically. 'And it does make for such a very thrilling and romantic story.'

★   ★   ★

'Poor Julian,' said Lizzie when, a few minutes later Julian had put a hand to his brow and told them his nerves were in such a state of sensitivity, he must return home immediately. 'It was very brave of him, to have cussed at his attackers when they were so fierce.'

'I don't believe he did any such thing,' said Tom. 'I think it more likely, he cowered in his saddle and said, 'Take anything you like, only don't hurt my precious person, I beg.'' Tom went on in a high pitched, totally hopeless impression of Julian's carefully modulated tones. He gave a sidelong glance at Harry who frowned back at him. 'I'll wager Julian said, 'Take this too, it's a mere trumpery, a love token only, but you may have it, only leave me to go on my way.''

Lizzie giggled. 'Oh Tom, you are so droll.'

'Enough,' Harry said with a quick look in Sophie's direction. 'The poor fellow was obviously distressed.'

'Yes, obviously,' agreed Lizzie, quickly straightening her face. 'And whilst his horsemanship may leave a lot to be desired, he is so undeniably handsome.'

'Oh, I do so agree,' Sophie whispered.

'I wouldn't say so,' Tom said scowling. 'I always find him a dreadful bore, myself.'

'It's not his fault he's so lily-livered,' Lizzie went on. 'But I'm nearly sure if I had been in his boots, I should have been swooning with terror too.'

'Not you,' Tom said stoutly. 'In all probability you would have no problem out-riding them.'

'But they had pistols.'

Tom didn't reply.

'They took five guineas too — hardly a paltry sum.'

'Well, that's a lie,' Tom broke off, red-faced. 'Well, stands to reason — must be a lie. Julian coming back from a card party plump in the pocket? He's trying to bamboozle us!'

Lizzie grinned. 'I expect you're right, Tom. Julian was always one to embellish a tale — it's the poet in him. He can't help himself, can he, Harry?'

But Harry wasn't listening. 'You're exceedingly quiet, Sophie,' he said.

'Pleasant change,' Tom commented with a smirk.

Sophie gave a pale imitation of a smile as it occurred to her that the love token Julian had been robbed of was, in all probability, the lock of her own, very distinctive, pale auburn hair.

*　*　*

'That settles it,' pronounced Lady Isobel.

It was later in the afternoon, and the riding party had gathered together in the small sitting room at Ellington Park, and were presently waiting for a dish of tea to be brought by way of refreshment. Sophie and Lizzie had lost no time at all in telling Lady Isobel what an adventure had befallen Julian.

'Three ruffians this time? Pistols as well? From now on you take a groom with you everywhere you go, Sophie, unless Harry or Tom is with you. And I'm sure if your dear mama were alive she would tell you the same, Lizzie.'

'Yes, m'lady,' Lizzie replied. 'Although I'm sure there are no more Highwaymen to be seen in this area. They concentrate on the main highways only. And after all, we are a considerable way from Enfield.'

Lady Isobel smiled the manner of smile that brooked no disagreement. 'Yes, Lizzie, my love, I'm sure that's the common view, but please believe me, I would be failing in my duty as your late mother's friend if I did not persuade you to take notice of my words.'

'Entirely at your service, Lizzie. Only too happy to accompany you whenever and wherever you wish,' volunteered Tom.

'Never fear,' said Harry, frowning at his sister. 'We are grateful for your advice, and I will see Lizzie abides by it, but I beg you do not pay too much regard to Julian's stories.'

Sophie took a sharp intake of breath. 'You go too far, Harry. Are you saying that Julian made the whole thing up?'

Harry regarded her from under lazy

eyelids. 'No, merely that we know he is possessed of a highly active imagination.'

'It is the outside of enough, Harry. You and Tom have been poking fun at Julian for no good reason for long enough now. I was never so ashamed of the both of you. He has a sensitive nature, it's true, but maybe it would be no bad thing were you to cultivate a little more consciousness of the feelings of others.'

Lady Isobel's glance took in Sophie's flushed impassioned countenance then tarried a little longer on Harry's stolid expression of firm impassivity.

'Pray, if there's any more to tell Harry — do so . . . ' There was a long pause during which Lady Isobel's bright eyes never wavered from Harry's equally unflinching return stare. 'It seems not,' she went on after a light laugh. 'Well, meanwhile I count on you and Tom to look after Sophie and Lizzie in a way that is fitting. Might I rely on you for that?'

Both men assured her that indeed she could.

'Good,' Lady Isobel said with a charming smile. 'Now I may be comfortable . . . Sophie, my love, see what has become of the tea I ordered.'

Obediently, Sophie left the room only to discover when she was not three paces out of it, a footman coming towards her complete with a tray of tea and biscuits. She turned just outside the door and then paused before eventually re-entering.

In the background she could just hear the murmur of Tom and Lizzie laughing together over some shared jest, and then the light, amused tones of her mother.

'Those Highwaymen whoever, or wherever they may be, did you a dis-service, Harry.'

'Did me a dis-service? How might that be?'

Lady Isobel gave a tinkling laugh. 'I can't help but feel it a very great shame that they chose Julian as a victim . . . It

111

puts him once more in the light of a veritable hero — does it not — Harry?' She looked up with a smile as Sophie re-entered the room closely followed by the tray-bearing footman. 'Ah, how lovely . . . Sophie, sit beside Harry and pour some refreshment.'

Sophie did as she was bid, wondering whatever had happened to the laughing, open-faced Harry she had known all her life, to change him into this solemn-faced stranger. A stranger in Harry's skin, still with the same familiar thick brown hair and wearing the same understated clothes, but now with a new set to his jaw and the warmth in his hazel eyes suddenly turned to steely disapproval.

7

For some unaccountable reason, it seemed to Sophie that, over the next few days, both Tom and Harry and yes, even Lizzie, were avoiding her. Tom, it transpired, was only too happy to take his mother at her word and spend every waking hour, when he was not engaged upon estate business, enquiring whether he could be of service in escorting Lizzie on any visits or excursions in the neighbourhood.

Harry however, showed none of the same solicitous attitude towards Sophie. 'I trust you will let me know if I can be of service,' he had said, addressing a point somewhere just over her left shoulder as though there was nothing he'd like less. Unhappily, Sophie nodded in reply and hurriedly left the room before her expression could give away how miserable she felt.

It wasn't until Sunday, when she was idly watching the reflections of the stained glass church windows on the sleeve of Lord Horton's coat of blue superfine, that she remembered seeing him furtively searching the library shelves. The remainder of the service passed in a blur as Sophie did some rapid calculations.

The dinner to be held by Count and Countess Frimlington at Clayborough Manor was due to take place in two days' time, and Sophie knew with a sickening certainty that Lady Isobel would be unable to resist wearing the sapphire necklace. And the very next day was the day she knew Felix was due to leave for Ireland, and preparations were being made already. Suppose he secretly watched Lady Isobel retrieve the necklace from its hiding place? Suppose he were to take the sapphire necklace with him to London with all the temptations of its many gaming hells, on his way to Ireland?

Sophie knew she must confide her

worst fears to Tom without delay.

That same Sunday evening, at Lord and Lady Horton's invitation, the rector and his son and daughter, as friends of long standing, were invited to dine quite informally at Ellington Park. Sophie decided this must make no difference, she would lose no time in voicing her worries to Tom.

Dressed in a dark blue gown which she knew became her, Sophie resolved she must be at all times the pleasant, congenial dinner companion that ladies of quality aspired to become. She was seated next to Tom and opposite Harry, who had Lizzie as his neighbour.

The dinner invitation, being of a casual nature, did not include Julian and his parents, a fact for which Sophie was very grateful, though she did wonder why she had chosen the flattering blue gown when she knew full well Julian would not be a member of the party.

Lizzie was vivacious in a gown of burgundy, which set off her dark hair and eyes to perfection, and Harry's square-shouldered figure was clad in a well-cut dark coat, white waistcoat, and black pantaloons. Sophie was so used to seeing him in buckskins, top boots and a nankeen jacket, that she felt quite shy and ill at ease with the smart figure across the table.

'Has your usually robust appetite deserted you?' Harry enquired, eyeing Sophie's hardly touched plate of boiled leg of lamb with spinach, before it was removed ready for the next course.

'Not at all,' rejoined Sophie in an attempt at convivial banter. 'Although Tom would, I know, have everyone believe I have a prodigious appetite, I normally partake of quite ladylike portions, I assure you — an elegant sufficiency, as Mama would say.'

Harry smiled, but it was a small, tight-lipped smile. From her right, Sophie could hear Tom and Lizzie laughing, which was all they seemed to do when they were together lately. Sophie shot them an annoyed glance.

Why should they be so continually happy when surely it was obvious that Harry was out of sorts with her for no reason at all that she could fathom? What right had they to go round looking so pleased with themselves? Surely a little more sensitivity would be in order?

Miserably Sophie lowered her glance to the new plate placed before her, which contained pigeon pie. Then, looking up, she found herself to be under the scrutiny of a pair of very fine hazel eyes which, nevertheless, held a slightly stunned expression.

'Why are you staring? Have I suddenly developed the measles?' Sophie asked, her newly assumed ladylike manners deserting her at a stroke.

'No Sophie, you haven't,' Harry replied with still the same glazed countenance. He cleared his throat. 'The notion suddenly came to me, I — I have never seen you in such good looks.'

'Oh,' Sophie said, suddenly feeling a

tide of heat suffusing her face and shoulders. 'Well . . . Just . . . Well — stop it. The staring, I mean. No wonder I can't eat, with you glaring at me all the time. It would put anyone off their food, besides being ill mannered in the extreme.'

Realising that her sentiments could and should have been expressed in a more delicate fashion she stopped short, wishing herself at Jericho or anywhere else but seated here under Harry's keen observation.

What had possessed everyone all of a sudden?

Julian acting out of character by galloping around the countryside like a crazy man, Tom flirting and giggling with Lizzie and Lizzie returning the favour; and now Harry telling her how well she was looking after all day treating her as though she were quite beyond the pale.

'Beg pardon,' said Harry, contrite now. 'It certainly won't happen again.'

For the rest of the meal, Harry kept

to his word, and somehow that wasn't quite what Sophie wanted either. She watched him from beneath lowered lids as he kept up an amusing conversation with Felix concerning horseflesh and Lady Isobel about the rival merits of paintings by Reynolds, Gainsborough and Romney; as well as including his father in a conversation which encompassed a few comments on Greek architecture. *Really*, thought Sophie. *Was there any topic on which Harry could not converse with consummate ease?*

Finally dinner was over and the gentlemen left to their port. Soon, however, they rejoined the ladies, and a rubber of whist was set up for the older generation while Tom suggested that the four younger members of the party go to the long gallery for a game of skittles.

At first Sophie was loath to join in, partly because she knew Lizzie and Harry would win, because they nearly always did. But also because she wanted, more than anything, to get away from this new, disturbing Harry, who was at one time so provoking and the next moment complimenting her looks! The whole idea of this last reality seemed so bizarre that Sophie almost persuaded herself it had never happened, and was merely some figment of her overactive imagination.

Nevertheless, this would be an ideal opportunity to voice her fears about Felix somehow taking possession of the necklace. Impatiently she watched as the skittles were set up at one end of the long gallery. Then she busied herself in making out the score cards, because that was what she always did, and watched Tom put a well-placed marker at the point the ladies were to bowl from.

'Tom — I must speak with you.'

'Eh?' Tom looked up from his careful positioning of a second marker further back, for the gentlemen.

'It's about my necklace — the sapphires.'

'What about them . . . ? Lizzie, I propose that you and I take on Harry and Sophie. That way at least I'll stand a chance.'

'Tom, only listen!' Sophie said, quite loudly this time.

Three pairs of eyes were directly turned towards her.

'All right. No need to throw a fit of the vapours — I'm listening,' Tom said with a high colour.

Half expecting them to be dismissive of her fears, Sophie explained how she'd come across Felix searching the library shelves, but immediately found she had the full attention of all three of them.

'Sad thing,' said Tom. 'I confess I used to like and respect my stepfather. Wizard on the racecourse — picked a winner every time. But now it seems his drinking and gaming have taken such a hold on him, and he is so liverish and forever anxious to return to the tables . . . Sadly, I think you have the right of it, Sophie. Believe we must take all steps to ensure the safety of those sapphires. I could see if I can prevail upon Mama not to wear the necklace.'

'Tom, she has a new gown with a blue brocade embroidered overskirt. The sapphires match it exactly, as well as matching her eyes, which she is particularly aware of . . . If Mama has a weakness, it is her vanity. She knows she looks well in the sapphires and loves to wear them. I'm very much afraid she will be unable to resist.'

'I'll speak with Mama,' said Tom. 'Now don't give us that Friday face, we're here to play skittles, are we not?'

No one would perceive, thought Sophie some fifteen minutes later, that all four laughing participants in the riotous game of skittles, in the long gallery, had anything on their minds other than obtaining the highest score.

★ ★ ★

The following morning, Sophie was not surprised when Tom and Lady Isobel spent a considerable time closeted together in her boudoir. Sophie sat in the morning room, her much-neglected embroidery by her, with the door ajar so she could pounce on Tom the moment he reappeared.

'Ah, Sophie,' he said, joining her in the morning room and carefully closing the door. 'Just spoke with Mama. And we've contrived what is an excellent plan.'

'Am I to comprehend that Mama listened?'

'Well, of course she listened, she knows I ain't one to kick up a dust for nothing. She also had misgivings about wearing the necklace and had planned to return it to its hiding place with full speed after wearing it. Told her what you'd seen. She was most distressed.'

'So will she make some excuse not to wear it? I know! I have a capital idea — she could say she's frightened of the Highwaymen in the area!' suggested an inspired Sophie.

'Eh? No, that would in no way

suffice. No Epping Highwayman would come so far afield as Clayborough Manor, you may be very sure of that. And our journey encompasses only the smallest stretch of road which could be classed as Highway. Besides, we'll have a driver and a footman in attendance. Felix would never stand that as an excuse. You know full well how by stealth and charm he invariably obtains his way with things. He'll insist Mama wears the sapphires, and it would be sadly out of character for her not to do so.'

'Well then,' Sophie said, turning away with a shrug of her shoulders, 'The necklace is lost. He will take it. I know he will.'

'On the day of the dinner, Mama, will fetch the necklace from the library long before Felix has risen. And when we return home, keeping her high necked cloak around her, Mama will plead the headache and go straight to her bedchamber. The plan is, she will have already passed the necklace to me in the darkness of the carriage! Then, taking very great care Felix is nowhere in sight, I will put the necklace in its hiding place. Felix will be watching Mama, not me. And when he notices its absence from her neck, she will say it was so heavy it brought on her headache and that's why she passed it to me a little earlier. Fait accompli! By that time it will be too late. He can hardly admit to wanting to 'borrow' the necklace in order to have a copy made.'

'You don't think he might try to make a scene and then demand the necklace regardless?'

Tom shook his head. 'Not his style. He is all that is charming on the surface, but devious and sly beneath. No, he'll give up on the necklace for the time being at least, and when he is gone to Ireland, I will lodge it with the bank in London and there it will stay until your marriage — you have my word on it.'

'Well, I hope you may be right,' Sophie said, remembering the greedy expression she had seen on Felix's features as he surreptitiously searched the library shelves.

* * *

It was not until the early morning of the day of the prestigious dinner at Clayborough Manor that Sophie had the time or inclination to consider Julian, and whether or not he'd made any lonely pilgrimages to the barn in order to leave a message for her. Although on the whole she thought it unlikely, she felt duty-bound to check before she met him again at the formal dinner party that evening.

She spent quite some minutes in composing a short note to leave beneath the stone.

J, she wrote. *It is not seemly or sensible to any more meet in this fashion. I look forward to enjoying your company in the presence of others at social events of the season. Your friend, Sophie.*

It seemed a little stiff, she thought,

but conveyed her sentiments with an exactitude she was happy to admit to. Because, although she had jumped to his defence and been truly upset to think of poor Julian being set upon by Highway robbers, she now realised that Julian, whilst having the appearance of a romantic hero, was one whose company she found humourless and — well — rather tedious.

Before she could change her mind, she dressed quickly in Tom's old riding breeches and a ruffled shirt, then slipped out through a side passage into the early morning air.

Her heart, she noticed, as she hacked her way across the familiar Ellington land, was not beating wildly at the thought of a possible encounter with Julian. It was more of a brisk heartbeat. The kind of heartbeat that said it was time to finish this rather foolish episode, put it behind her, and start afresh. And after all, now Julian was attending card parties and dinners with the cream of the county, the objective of cheering him up had in part been achieved. She regretted being foolish enough to part with a lock of her hair and her locket, but there was nothing to be done about that now it was nestling in the pocket of some common thief.

Sophie reached the barn and tethered Firefly outside, where he pawed the ground impatiently, whilst she confirmed that no message had been left for her. Somehow the prospect of explaining the contents of the note and engineering enough privacy to do so was daunting so, hoping very much that Julian would read it before she saw him at Clayborough Manor that evening, she placed her own note beneath the stone.

That done, her spirits lifted as she surveyed the dawn mists gradually rising with the warmth of the early morning sun. At the other side of the hill in a continuation of the nook that sheltered the barn, was a small still lake, where a punt was moored by a small rickety landing stage.

On impulse, Sophie turned Firefly's

head in this direction and set off at a controlled canter.

The lake looked the very picture of enchantment in the still, morning air. The oaks and elms in the background were clothed in fresh green hues, just tinged with pale rays of sunlight, and reflected themselves in the calm waters beneath.

Sophie's breath caught in her throat as she surveyed the scene before her. Despite always being aware of how privileged she was to live in such exquisite surroundings, the sheer magic of it all, washed over her anew as she sat astride Firefly staring before her.

She was brought out of her reverie by a small cough and, turning, saw Harry complete with fishing rod, a little to one side of the landing stage:

'Beautiful, isn't it?' he said.

Wishing she'd worn her favourite green riding habit instead of the woefully embarrassing breeches, Sophie nodded and dismounted. 'Too lovely a morning to stay in bed,' she agreed. She nodded at the keeper net. 'Caught anything yet?'

'No. I've come here to think, really. There are things I'm beholden to do, that I'm not entirely comfortable with doing . . . Just brought my rod for company, really.'

Effortlessly, Sophie squatted on the ground next to him. For a moment she felt herself a child again, at ease with her company and surroundings.

She gave a sigh.

'What was that for?'

Idly, Sophie threw a small pebble into the water and watched as the ripples spread. 'Oh, growing up, I suppose, and wishing we could stay children for ever.'

Harry chuckled. 'When you were a child, you were always wanting to be as old as Lizzie or as tall as Tom.'

'Yes, but somehow, as a child, you don't think of the complications that go with age.'

Harry clasped his hands round his knees. 'Surely Sophie, your life can't be so very complicated?'

'It's possible sometimes, Harry, to do silly, ill-judged things without quite foreseeing the consequences,' Sophie said, thinking of the lock of hair she'd given Julian.

Gravely, Harry considered her. 'Actions can often be undone, surely?'

'Not if one has been very foolish,' Sophie said in a small voice.

'None of us are perfect. We are all capable of foolish actions.'

'Not you, Harry. You are far too sensible.'

'Oh, am I?' Harry said softly, leaning closer. 'I'm boring, sensible old Harry, am I?'

The skin on Sophie's bare arm began to tingle. She looked down and saw Harry's long fingers were very close to her wrist. She wanted to move her arm away but found she couldn't.

There was the plop of a carp surfacing for air, the small stirring of a breeze in the trees — the whisper of a touch on her arm.

Harry's hand lifted her chin, forcing her to look at him. 'We can't stay children for ever,' he said. 'Decisions have to be made.' Gently his fingers traced the outline of her face.

Sophie stopped breathing, her eyes fascinated by the dimple at the side of his mouth. She tried to imagine what it would feel like to kiss that dimple, to have that slightly crooked mouth descend on hers. Wonderingly, her gaze travelled up and met his, which was steadily regarding her.

Then a magpie screeched and Harry blinked and almost imperceptibly moved away.

Face burning, Sophie scrambled to her feet. 'I must go.'

Harry laughed. 'Yes, you are all to dine out at Clayborough Manor tonight, I understand.'

Sophie nodded. 'But, you will be there too, won't you?'

Harry chuckled again. 'Sadly, no. Too grand an occasion by far for the Crightons, I'm afraid. Only Lords and double-barrelled names allowed through the door . . . That's the difference between us, Sophie. There are many doors open to you that for me, alas,' he put his hand on his heart in mock horror, 'will always be closed.'

'Harry, Tom is right. You do sometimes talk the most nonsensical rubbish,' said Sophie, grabbing Firefly's rein.

'Julian will be there, I expect?'

Sophie flushed slightly at Harry's directness. 'So I believe,' she replied 'You'll hardly miss me then. You will be able to feast your eyes on him all evening, dreaming dreams of romance.'

'Why would I do that? Anyway, it has nothing to do with you where my affections lie.'

Harry looked away, his eyes on a sparrow hawk that was slowly circling above them. 'Don't undervalue yourself, Sophie. Julian's not worthy of you.'

Then he smiled and came closer, linking his fingers for her booted foot. 'Have a care, Sophie,' he said, as he tossed her into the saddle.

8

The extravagance of a thousand candles, or so it seemed to Sophie, flooded out of Clayborough Manor casements, to mix with the golden glow of torches flaring from the Medieval sconces on the stone walls. Together they bathed the forecourt in a soft, all-encompassing light.

Alongside her brother, Sophie stood at the front steps waiting for their carriage to arrive. Lord and Lady Horton were saying their goodbyes to the Count and Countess and Sophie watched with admiration as Lady Isobel complimented their hosts prettily on the successful evening. Lord Horton remained in the background, quiet, well-mannered, and charm personified, as always.

The Stafford-Smythe party had already left. Julian had been resplendent in a new waistcoat, an intricately tied cravat, and a shirt with such high points he had difficulty in moving his head. Along with this, his air of passionate turbulence had been replaced by a wearied civility which, Sophie considered, bordered on the arrogant.

Regarding all this with a somewhat wry amusement, she concluded that Julian had abandoned his tousled poet persona for the more dandified appearance of a veritable tulip of fashion. Quietly, in passing, she'd asked if he had exercised his horses in the direction of Ellington Place recently. He'd considered her with an expression brimming over with ennui, and replied that he didn't think he had.

Her face burning slightly at such a set down, Sophie resolved to collect her unread message from beneath the stone in the barn and regretted that she'd spent even five minutes in its composition. But just then Julian had chosen to smile, and his face lit up with such beauty, it was hard to resist. Sophie could do nothing to resist and had to acknowledge that someone as handsome as Julian would always be forgiven the most boorish of behaviour, purely on the merit of the perfection of every one of his features.

And now, standing on the front steps of the Manor, she regretted that she'd spent so much time in pining over Julian — and even more, the loss of her locket, which had been given to her by an aunt of whom she'd been quite fond.

'Our carriage, Sophie,' Tom said in her ear. 'Now the jest begins.'

Sophie shot him a warning look because Felix was sauntering up to them. 'Hardly a jest,' she said. 'More a deception.'

But Tom's eyes were still dancing with amusement as he helped his sister into the carriage.

'I'll sit next to Tom, I know you dislike sitting with your back to the horses, Sophie,' Lady Isobel said. Sophie opened her mouth to demur, but found her mother's fingers were biting into her arm and realised immediately that of course Mama and Tom must sit together. 'Well, it was an entertaining enough evening, would you not agree, my love?' asked Lady Isobel of Felix, once they were all seated comfortably.

From his position in the seat next to Sophie, Felix gave a yawn. 'A trifle spinsterish,' he replied. 'Fellow keeps a good cellar, though. Must have brought the claret with him. Only shame is he didn't bring his own chef, I think I have the indigestion.'

Lady Isobel was immediately all concern. 'Are you not feeling quite the thing? I perceived you to look a little liverish once or twice this evening. I must confess I found the food to be a trifle rich myself, and feel the inkling of a headache coming on . . . I think I shall shut my eyes a little and rest. Perhaps you should do the same.'

Clever Mama, thought Sophie. Felix with his eyes closed, the planted suggestion of her own headache to come. The perfect setting for the passing of the sapphires to Tom. She gave an exaggerated yawn. 'I think I might just close my eyes for a little too,' she said, determined to play her part in the ruse.

'Not much company to be enjoyed here then,' Tom said, grinning. 'I was hoping to seek your opinion of Julian's new mode of dress. He was trussed up like a turkey, and those yellow clocks on his stockings! The man's a jest — he don't need to speak. His clothes and bearing say it all. Can't abide the fellow — never could! ... Five guineas, indeed! The day Julian wins five guineas at the card table is the day I'll cease playing!' He chuckled. 'Good entertainment value, though. I thought I should lose countenance several times when he forgot the height of his shirt collar and very nearly lost an eye ... Oh dear, oh dear!'

Tom mumbled on to himself in this fashion for several minutes before realising that he was obtaining no response other than the steady snoring of Lord Horton.

Sophie strained her eyes in the shadowy interior of the coach but failed to see any discernible movement which might signify her mother's passing of the sapphires to Tom.

Then she found that in spite of all, she must have dosed a little because suddenly she was jerked awake by a thump on the roof and a shout, followed by particularly rough patch of road, where the carriage tipped and swayed alarmingly.

'Overhanging branch,' Tom said dismissively.

Lord Horton snorted himself awake. 'Damn driver,' he said under his breath. Then firmly closed his eyes again. The driver soon had the carriage under control again but Sophie remained alert and wakeful against the cushioned interior.

Within another few minutes, there was a further kerfuffle and the carriage lurched to a halt. Sophie's head jerked forward, and Lord Horton almost lost his seat and landed on the floor of the carriage.

'What the devil? . . . ' exclaimed Felix, hauling himself back in position.

'We must have a wheel loose,' Tom said.

There was the sound of confusion outside. The horses were jostling one another, the carriage sides swayed, and there was the sound of rough language in a harsh, unrecognisable voice.

Sophie's eyes grew wide — something was clearly amiss. She glanced across at her brother. Tom's face was tense, his eyes on the door of the carriage. Even as she looked the door opened and the nose of a pistol poked through.

'Stand and deliver!' said a harsh, menacing voice.

★ ★ ★

Lord Horton gave a muttered oath. 'Oh surely not again,' he said. 'The very audaciousness of it. This is hard to tolerate!'

'We don't have much choice in the matter,' Lady Isobel replied shakily. 'But fortunately we have nothing of value this time. So this gentleman may go about his business.'

'Come on now, m'lady,' rasped the Highwayman. 'Let's 'ave yer geegaws.'

'Well, I have a ring,' Lady Isobel said more calmly. 'But if you remember, we had only a few trinkets the last time you stopped us, and certainly have no more now. We have been dining with friends of long acquaintance — an informal occasion. And of course since we were once before robbed — as well you know — we are careful of what we bring with us.'

She extended fingers that were not quite steady, and the Highwayman stretched across to take the two rings she was wearing.

'And you, sir,' he said to Tom. 'I'll wager that's a diamond pin you are wearing and a gold fob at yer waist, so be 'anding 'em over while the lady unhooks the necklace she's sure to be clutching at under that cloak she has around her throat.'

Sophie's heart, which had been beating rather faster than usual, now started to pound quite alarmingly. Had Mama had time to pass the necklace to Tom? Tom was strangely quiet. Staring at the Highwayman through slightly narrowed eyes he nodded in Lady Isobel's direction. 'You'd best do as he says, Mama,' he said curtly, then fixed his attention on Felix.

'This thievery is insupportable,' Felix said in a dangerously quiet voice with no vestige of charm left in it. 'And you will pay for it, sir!'

Taking the sapphires with his free hand, the Highwayman laughed.

'Where is the driver? Where the footman?' went on Lord Horton in the same quiet menacing voice.

''Fraid, sir, they took a little tumble, some ways back,' said the Highwayman. 'Now if you'd just like to empty yer pockets . . . I'll not trouble the little lady — I'll be gone.'

Felix felt inside his pocket, but instead of pulling out a purse of silver, he pulled out a small pearl-handled pistol. Sophie gasped loudly, cowering in fear. There was a shot and the acrid smell of gunpowder filled the inside of the carriage.

'My God!' The carriage rocked as Tom leapt to his feet. 'You fool, Felix! You could have killed us all.'

The Highwayman, swaying slightly, staggered away from the carriage and disappeared into the trees.

'If you had not stood in my way, you pudding-hearted dolt, I would have killed the scoundrel without a doubt,' Felix said in a voice that was still quiet but as deadly as steel.

'I'm going after him,' Tom shouted, grabbing the pistol and jumping from the coach. 'And I must go back and find Barlow and the poor young footman. I would never have thought this to happen on this road.'

'Oh Tom, have a care,' entreated Lady Isobel, whose face was now deathly white.

Sophie discovered herself to be shaking. It occurred to her that perhaps being robbed wasn't exactly the exciting adventure she had thought. It had all happened so quickly, she could scarce remember it. Because of the precariousness of the carriage ride earlier, she had accepted without question that all that was amiss was a loose wheel. She hadn't even had a clear glimpse of the Highwayman who, far from flirting with her, had ignored her completely.

After Tom had disappeared into the trees in pursuit of his quarry, the three occupants of the carriage sat in silence for a while, seemingly too stunned to speak

'I'm sorry, my love. It seems we have lost your inheritance,' said Lady Isobel eventually, in a trembling voice.

'Mama, how can you say that, when you might have been killed? Suppose that oaf had fired back? It was you who were in the line of fire, not my stepfather!' Sophie bestowed a scorching glance in the direction of Felix. 'Then I should have been truly an orphan . . . '

'I perceive you are determined to make a drama out of this,' said Lord Horton in a bored voice. 'Your mother was never in danger, Sophie; everyone knows Highwaymen don't shoot, they merely threaten. If that brainless brother of yours hadn't stood up, we would have a dead Highwayman and the sapphires still. But no; Tom's so caper-witted he had to interfere. Ah well, the sapphires are gone, there's nought to be done. You were foolish, Isobel, to wear the sapphires at all.'

'I recall it was you who insisted I should wear them — to impress the Count, you said! No doubt, in order for you to obtain a loan from him on a future occasion!'

Sophie gasped, Mama must be upset; she had never heard her address Felix in such a manner before.

Lord Horton's eyes glittered dangerously but further conversation was cut short by the sound of Tom's return together with Old Barlow the driver, and a very frightened under-footman. Tom looked extremely grim.

'This lad travels in the carriage and I suggest he takes a sip of brandy from your flask, Felix. I'll travel up top with Old Barlow who's a bit shaken up. Oh, one thing, Mama, your rings and my pin and fob have been found. He must have dropped them as he fled.'

'The necklace?' Sophie asked tremulously.

Tom shook his head. 'No, he must have kept a tight hold on that.'

Lord Horton sighed. 'He can't have got far. I'm surprised at your being unable to apprehend him, I winged him in the shoulder, you know.'

Tom ignored him. 'I suggest we get home as soon as may be,' he said brusquely. 'My mother and my sister need to recover from this ordeal.'

* ★ * ★ * ★

By the time they arrived at Ellington Place, Sophie was beginning to think she truly did suffer from the headache she had quite made up earlier. Lord Horton alighted the carriage and took the stone steps, to the imposing front door, two at a time, Tom close behind. Sophie would have attempted to keep up but Lady Horton put a restraining hand on her arm. Alarmed at just how strained was her mother's face, Sophie, her skirts held high in one hand, stopped half way up the steps. 'Mama?' Tom looked round and retraced his steps to stand beside them.

Lady Isobel spoke rapidly in a soft voice. 'Sophie, your mother is a very foolish woman, but I am come to my senses. You are to say you are tired and have the headache after all the excitement and must go to your bed. Thankfully your stepfather will see nothing strange in that happening now.'

'I must go directly to the stables,

Mama,' interrupted Tom urgently.

'No Tom, you must not! You must stay here with Felix and me, and act your part of outrage and shock . . . No Tom,' as Tom's jaw stuck out belligerently and he opened his mouth to remonstrate, 'on this you will do as I say — to do anything else would be sure to arouse Felix's suspicions. Now, catch your stepfather up, I beg you.'

Sophie looked on in bewilderment as, after a last enquiring glance at his mother, Tom obeyed.

'Now help me up these steps, Sophie, as though I'm an old woman ready for her deathbed scene which, believe me, I might well be before tonight is eventually out.'

'But Mama, I don't understand,' Sophie, said feeling as though she'd strayed somehow into a play with no script to follow.

'Once you have made your excuses to Felix, you are to take some brandy — go immediately by the side passage to the stables. There or thereabouts you will find Robin . . . ' Lady Isobel gave a wan smile. 'You have always had a yearning for romantic adventure, have you not? Oh, how your brother persuaded me to this I'll not fathom . . . ' Her words trailed off as they entered the large marble-floored hall.

'This calls for brandy all round,' went on Lady Isobel in a feeble but carrying voice. 'We have all had a shock to the system.'

Mrs Cope was standing in the shadow of the majestic staircase. 'My Lady, Robin would like a word.'

'Mama, allow me to see Robin in your stead,' offered Tom.

Lady Isobel's brows arched. 'No Tom that will not do at all,' she said softly but with great emphasis. 'You and I must stay here with your stepfather and discuss this evening's catastrophe. Sophie, you must go to bed — you look completely done in.'

Sophie opened her mouth in order to protest, then suddenly realised that her mother was looking at her with such an expression of entreaty on her face that she could not argue. 'Goodnight, Mama,' she said and watched helplessly as Lord and Lady Horton followed by Tom, went into the library.

★ ★ ★

'Here, Miss Sophie.' Mrs Cope thrust a bottle of brandy into Sophie's hands and wrapped her cloak more firmly round her. 'You go now with Robin, you'll find him at the side passage door . . . I don't know what my Lady's thinking of to mix you up in all this. This was used to be such a respectable house, and now there's all these goings-on. What your father would have to say to the matter I cannot countenance! Well, no good me rattling on — best get to the stables like your mama told you.'

Sophie looked from the bottle of brandy in her hand to Mrs Cope's face and back again.

'But why?' she started, then stopped

as she saw Robin peer anxiously round the corner of the hall. When he saw Sophie, he instantly faded back into the shadows.

'Robin, just what is all this?' asked Sophie breathlessly, as she caught up with him at the entrance to the stables. 'And why are you carrying half Mrs Cope's linen cupboard with you?'

'It's all right, Miss Sophie, you'll understand in a jiffy.' Robin pushed open the door of the far barn in the stables.

There was a dim light at the far end of the barn. Cautiously, at first Sophie went towards it. A lantern was set on the straw-covered floor and next to it was a recumbent form, which even as she gazed, moved, groaned and struggled to sit up. Heart beating with the impossibility of what she was seeing, Sophie drew closer.

The outline of a head turned towards her. Out of a pale face, a pair of hazel eyes looked straight into hers, then lost their focus as a swoon took him over.

'H-H-Harry?' whispered an unbelieving Sophie.

But Harry didn't answer; instead he slumped over into the surrounding straw like a dead man.

9

'Harry, Harry, open your eyes. Don't you dare die!' With not a care for her very best gown, Sophie had flung herself down on her knees on the straw beside him. She cradled him against her and looked over his head at Robin. 'He's not going to die — is he?' she asked in a shaky voice.

'No, not 'im. Master Harry's always been a tough 'un. He'll be right as a trivet once we staunch the bleeding and bandage him up good an' tight.'

'Bleeding? Oh, no!' Sophie stared at the dark patch on the shoulder of Harry's coat.

'Fraid he's lost a lot of blood. The shot didn't penetrate, but he's still got a shoulder wound as'll give him a stiff neck and arm for a while . . . It's the loss of blood making him weak. Here, see if you can get 'im to take some

153

brandy, we'll need 'im to co-operate like, if we're to get this coat and shirt off him now.'

Wordlessly, Sophie did as she was told and managed to pour some of the fiery liquid down Harry's throat. But his eyes remained tight shut during the struggle to remove his jacket, which luckily was old, loose-cut and hardly the style of coat he normally wore.

'This isn't Harry's coat,' Sophie commented grimly.

'No,' agreed an equally grim-faced Robin. 'One of the Rector's old gardening coats, I'll be bound.'

Between them, Sophie and Robin removed his bloodstained waistcoat then ripped the shirt from Harry's shoulder. He winced where the drying blood had stuck the linen fast to his body. Sophie carefully bathed the cloth away from the skin beneath and, trying not to look at Harry's broad and manly chest more than was decorous, cleaned the wound and dabbed brandy on to it.

Harry winced and let out a curse.

'Glad you ain't turning sickly on me, Miss Sophie, though you always was full of spunk. Hold that pad tight now,' instructed Robin, 'while I tear this sheet for bandages.' He got to his feet and went to fetch the sheet, which he'd flung down near the barn entrance.

Harry cursed and his eyelids fluttered open. 'Sophie,' he murmured. 'Thought it was you . . . Got your sapphires — all nice and tight.'

'My sapphires? Oh, Harry, I don't care a rush for my sapphires . . . '

Harry had to close his eyes once again, his face still a ghastly white.

'Harry, Harry, open your eyes — I can't bear to see you so pale.'

A couple of hot teardrops landed on Harry's bare torso. Obediently he opened one eye and attempted a crooked smile. 'Well, this is a fine thing, Sophie . . . Thought you'd like yer geegaws,' he attempted the rasping voice of the Highwayman but it came out little above a whisper. He swallowed painfully. 'Any more brandy available?

Seems to help me think.'

Wiping away her tears with the back of her hand, Sophie held the brandy bottle against Harry's mouth.

'That's better,' Harry stretched out his good arm and reached up to touch her wet cheek. Then his arm dropped again as though the effort was too much, and draped itself around her shoulders. 'Don't go all mawkish on me now, Sophie. Only a flesh wound, do assure you. Ain't going to die!'

'Don't say that, Harry. I can't bear to contemplate it even as a jest.' Despite all her efforts to the contrary a few more tears spilled out of Sophie's eyes. 'And of course I'm upset, for I care about you just as well as I care for my brother . . . Well, more, actually, because Tom is so excessively aggravating on occasion . . . ' She broke off as Harry's good arm suddenly tightened round her.

'Care for you too Sophie . . . Too much . . . Not like a sister at all. I mean brother . . . ' He pulled her head down and brushed her lips softly with his own. Then stared deeply into her eyes. 'Cannot be, though; cannot be.' His arm went slack and his head rolled to the side.

'Passed out,' Robin said from just outside the circle of the lantern's light. 'Just as well. We need to get him bandaged up.'

The two of them worked quietly on the prostrate form. Then Robin gently draped a horse blanket over him.

'I'll stay here with him tonight,' Robin said in answer to Sophie's unasked question. 'Though I'm expecting that brother of yours any time soon.'

'He's been delayed,' Sophie said shortly. 'Don't let him disturb Harry, will you? Make him keep quiet and not tease him about anything.'

Robin chuckled. 'Mr Harry won't be waking for a good few hours yet, he's sleeping like a babe in arms. Oh, I've sent a stable lad to the Rectory to tell them Mr Harry stays here tonight. The

Rector will no doubt think he's with your brother in the middle of a card game or some such thing.'

'Thank you, Robin,' Sophie said, watching Harry frown in his sleep. 'I know we can rely on you to be discreet. Oh, and Robin, I pray you will disregard anything you heard Mr Harry saying. He was quite unaware, you see, of — well, he didn't mean . . . It was all a nonsense . . . '

'Well, Miss, I know as it's not my place, but there's them that think very highly of Mr Harry . . . Surprised it's him as is in this scrape, not your brother. Not that there's anything he wouldn't do for you and Master Tom, and I dare say that's what it comes down to. And you two, more often or not, scrapping and at each other's throats, aggravating an' teasing an' the like. And Mr Harry sorting it out and making you friends again. You and Mr Harry was born to be together, and that's a fact.'

Sophie drew herself up to her full

height. 'I'd be obliged if you didn't talk such addle-brained nonsense, Robin.'

'Right you are, my lady,' replied Robin, belatedly recalling Sophie's correct form of address.

Sophie turned and picked up Harry's bloodstained waistcoat and the Rector's jacket, which looked to be beyond repair, and felt the weight of the necklace in one of its pockets. 'I'll take this,' she said. 'Tom will bring one of his own shirts and a jacket for Mr Harry's use, I'm sure . . . Goodnight, Robin. And thank you!'

'It's nothing, my lady,' Robin said, his face carefully expressionless.

Sophie returned to the house and reached the sanctuary of her bedchamber without further incident. Once there, she felt in the pocket of the coat, withdrew the sapphire necklace and secreted it beneath her pillow. Then, frowningly, she explored the inside pocket of Harry's plain, buff waistcoat. There was something round and flat, like an over-large coin nestling within.

Wonderingly, she pulled out the locket containing her hair that she'd given to Julian, what felt like years ago.

A tide of heat swept from her feet to the top of her head as she realised what must have happened. Not only had Harry somehow allowed himself to be persuaded into this mad scheme of masquerading as a Highwayman, in order to keep the sapphires from falling into the hands of her stepfather; he'd also, no doubt egged on by Tom, held up Julian and found the locket to be amongst his valuables. Did he imagine she had given the locket to Julian as a love token? Of course, what else was he to think when Julian had described it as such himself? Burning with humiliation, Sophie sat down on her bed, feeling sick and ashamed. No wonder he had been so distant with her. Harry must think her quite a trollop.

What was even more disturbing was that whereas once she would have laughed at such a notion, she now found herself to be dismayed by the idea that Harry's good opinion of her was in such jeopardy.

Wonderingly, Sophie held the waistcoat in her hands, then, on sudden impulse, buried her nose in the cloth and breathed in Harry's smell. Oh, how she loved that smell.

Oh, how she loved Harry!

She sat, still as a statue, while the enormity of her feelings spread throughout her body. She couldn't do, could she? Not in a pounding heart, dry mouthed kind of way? Not Harry?

'Harry, I love you,' she said softly. 'Of course, of course, I do.'

A sudden tear spilled onto her hot cheek. Suppose, just suppose, Harry did not return her feelings?

★ ★ ★

After a restless night, Sophie rose early determined to go straight to the stables. First she took time to hide the sapphires in the toe of one of her old riding boots, and to bundle the old clothes up and place them at the back of an unused drawer. She could find a way to dispose of those later. Harry must be hungry by now.

Without stopping to work out a plan, she went straight to the kitchens and took a basket of bread and some ham and cheese, covered it with a cloth and walked swiftly down the servants' passage to the side door.

'Tom!'

'Oh capital, Sophie!' said Tom who was just coming in by the side door. 'Forgot about food! I'll take that to Harry!'

Sophie was so concerned that she hardly protested as Tom took the basket from her. She fell into step beside him. 'Is he all right?'

'Course he's all right! Hardly a scratch. He's just a bit stiff and says he could eat a horse.'

'Oh.' Sophie took another look at her brother, whose appearance was dishevelled to say the least. 'You slept the night in the stables, I presume?'

'Well — least I could do. Wasn't worried, mind you. Just wondered what Lizzie might say if she found out Harry had been hurt and I was the cause.'

'I thought it must be your ill-judged idea . . . '

They were walking together towards the stables now and suddenly a blinding fury overtook Sophie. 'Whatever were you thinking of, Tom? — and Mama too? For I perceive she must have been in on the plot. Harry nearly killed — for a necklace!'

'You always was a wildcat female, but never took you for a pea goose, Sophie. Harry wasn't nearly killed — it was the merest scratch! Capital lark! He'll be right as a trivet in a day or so. No need to go acting like a wet goose and turning mawkish like he's the love of your life.'

'I'll be mawkish if I choose to, and happen I do love him! Of course I love him,' said Sophie warming to her theme. 'Like a brother. Well, like any other brother but you! If he dies,

163

Thomas Gregory Ellington, I'll never be able to forgive you!'

Tom stared at his sister's vehement face. 'Steady on, Sophie. Stop having the vapours. Won't help Harry to have a hysterical female weeping all over him, will it?'

'You're the most hateful of brothers and I am not weeping,' said Sophie wiping her eyes with the edge of her shawl.

'So I see.' Tom regarded Sophie quizzically and paused at the door of the old barn. 'Now, no Friday faces. Harry thinks you're a brave, true heroine, so try and behave so.'

Sophie didn't answer; she was too busy wondering if what Tom had just said could possibly be true.

★   ★   ★

Sophie and Tom returned to the house in time to join Lord Horton for breakfast. Pleading a headache, Sophie sat at the far end of the table and helped herself only to a small repast of ham and eggs. As usual, Tom piled his plate high, then embarked on a largely unanswered conjecture as to the present whereabouts of last night's Highwayman and, more to the point, the exact location of the missing sapphires.

'Lord,' said Tom, for maybe the fourth time, 'I just wish I could lay my hands on him! But he'll be half ways to Newcastle by now, no doubt.'

Lord Horton raised a weary eyebrow. 'Tom, I am heartily sick of the word Highwayman and your opinion of where he may be. The likelihood of our ever setting eyes on him or the family sapphires again is exceeding remote. I wish you would kindly refrain from mentioning the matter again before I leave for Ireland!'

'Beg pardon sir,' said Tom, immediately all contrition. 'Didn't mean to upset you. Wouldn't do that for the world. Only meant to say that, well, these Highwaymen, they have escape routes, I've heard, and they have friends too ... Didn't mean to aggravate though, 'pon my word . . . '

Felix pushed his chair from the table. 'I have things to attend to before I leave. I plan to be away for at least a month, but taking all things into consideration I might extend my stay. I trust you will look to your mother while I am gone and seek the advice of the estate manager on all business matters as they arise?'

'Yes sir,' Tom answered in a dutiful manner, which belied the sparkle lurking in his eyes.

★   ★   ★

In the event, Lord Horton left for Liverpool, from where he would cross to Ireland, a little before noon. He intended to make enquiries in Liverpool, he said, about any sapphires recently come upon the market. Lady Isobel, who had appeared by this time, ventured that it might be considered a little early to hear anything of them yet. She thought the necklace would not make an appearance for a good few weeks — and that even then, it would have been broken up ready to be sold abroad.

Lord Horton's expression darkened and his lips twitched, but he bade Lady Isobel goodbye quite charmingly, trusting that her children would look after her and give no cause for concern in his absence. Thinking of the necklace sitting snugly in the toe of her old riding boot, Sophie's lips nearly formed a smile, but just in time she managed them back into an expression of almost tearful remorse.

With the departure of Lord Horton the whole of Ellington Place seemed to relax and unwind.

Lady Isobel heaved an audible sigh of relief and asked for some ratafia, cordial and biscuits to be brought to the library. Sophie sped up the long staircase, retrieved the sapphires from the toe of her boot and took them, wrapped in her shawl, to the library.

Together she watched with her

mother as Tom put the necklace back, where it belonged, behind the panelling in the library shelves.

'Thank goodness,' said Lady Isobel. 'It will be lodged in the bank in London before Felix returns. Now Tom, you may fetch Harry so that I can thank him adequately for his part in all this.'

'Yes,' agreed Sophie heartily. 'For I hardly had time to wish him good morning, when Tom chivvied me to move and appear at the breakfast table before my stepfather.'

There was a tap on the door and in a coat of Tom's that was a little tight on him, Harry, albeit walking a little stiffly, appeared before them. He still wore a pallor that made Sophie's heart quite turn over, but his eyes were twinkling in the same old Harry-ish way.

'How can I ever thank you?' said Lady Isobel, catching at his hands and leading him to a comfortable chair. 'And how can you forgive me for putting you in so much danger? Your father would never speak to me again if he knew what we had been at.'

'Well, just as well he don't know, and has no way of finding out,' Harry said with a grin.

'We are all sworn to secrecy, Mama,' said Tom. 'Robin and Mrs Cope only think some boyish dare or other was committed, and they are loyal and will say nothing. Barlow the driver, and the young footman, I've also paid handsomely to keep their own counsel. Told them we will have a paste replica of the necklace made if it can't be recovered, but naturally don't wish to advertise the fact. Lord Horton is gone to Ireland and by the time he returns, no one will remember the details. It could not have been executed any better.'

'Well, I just wish someone had thought to inform me,' Sophie said indignantly. 'How was I supposed to know what was happening?'

Lady Isobel smiled. 'Oh, my love,' she said. 'Your reactions were so perfect. You were frightened, but very brave. Then, when Felix was stupid enough to fire his pistol, you were so very angry. Because of you, he never suspected a thing for a moment. Then afterwards you went to the barn and assisted Robin in such a stalwart manner . . . We could not have done so well without you. But don't you see, if you had known about Harry, there would have been no containing you, and all would have been lost!'

'But Harry, how did you do it?' Sophie asked after a few moments of trying to decide whether to continue being affronted or to let her natural curiosity have the upper hand.

Harry grinned. 'I confess I wasn't completely happy about it, but after holding up Julian — we had intended to inform him of the jest, but when he said there were three of us and we'd taken five guineas from him when in truth we'd taken nothing, just given him a good roasting . . .'

'Well, the fellow deserved it,' interrupted Tom. 'Accusing me of cheating at cards!'

Harry's eyes twinkled. 'I have to agree with Tom, it was a capital jest . . . Then Lady Isobel said, 'Wouldn't it be perfect if Felix could be persuaded that the sapphires had been stolen?' And well, the rest just fell into place.' Harry took a sip of cordial and bit into a biscuit.

'But how did you do it all alone?' Sophie asked.

'Well, the plan was Tom's. We looked at the route the carriage would take and discovered a low overhanging branch. I tied my horse there, sat on the branch and waited . . . I gave a shout before booting Barlow and the boy off their perch, then drove on for half a mile before stopping. The horses were glad of the rest after carrying six people so far. The remainder you know. 'Come on milady — let's see yer geegaws',' he added, with a rasp in his voice.

Sophie smiled faintly. 'Yes, but when you were shot! Lord, you could have been killed, Harry!'

'Nonsense, he missed my heart by a mile.'

'Not your shoulder, though; and you had still to get home.'

'Well, yes, home was the original destination, but Tom came after me, half carried me back to my horse, got me on to him and we decided the Ellington stables was the best place to get patched up. Robin has helped us out of many a scrape before — we knew we could count on him.'

'Talking of which,' put in Lady Isobel. 'Harry, just as soon as you are refreshed enough, Sophie and Tom will escort you home.'

'Please don't feel obliged,' Harry said. 'I'm quite capable of riding alone — do assure you!'

'I'm coming with you — goes without saying,' said Tom.

'I'm coming too,' said Sophie feeling suddenly too shy to look Harry directly in the face, and very aware that her heart was beating in the strangest way.

10

Trying to swallow her feelings of frustration and annoyance, Sophie sat in the sewing room with her red-gold head bent over her embroidery. It was early afternoon and she knew she would be hard put to pass the hours until it was time for tea, then the remaining hours before dinner was served and, actually, all the hours that would make up the rest of her life. She sighed.

Holding a piece of parchment in her hand, Lady Isobel glided into the room. 'No, my love, don't disturb yourself,' she said as Sophie sprang to her feet. 'I am only come to tell you, that it seems your stepfather will remain in Ireland for considerably longer than first anticipated.'

Unsure how to react to this news, because although her mother was not exactly smiling, nor did she look to be upset, Sophie settled for, 'Oh?'

'Yes, it seems he has had a fall from his horse.'

Sophie gave a gasp. 'The accident was of a fatal nature?'

Lady Isobel's eyebrows lifted a notch. 'Surely you don't mean to wish him dead, my love?'

'Well of course, not dead precisely,' amended Sophie hurriedly. 'Just incapacitated enough to make it compulsory for him to stay away in Ireland almost indefinitely.'

Her mother consulted the letter further. 'Difficult to tell if that's the case . . . Lord knows, Sophie, I don't wish your stepfather ill — just in Ireland where he can't damage the Ellington estates. But I must confess, if he is confined to his bed until Tom reaches five and twenty, it would be a heartfelt relief.'

Sophie pretended to turn back to her embroidery and Lady Isobel lowered herself gracefully onto the settle beside her. 'All alone again, Sophie; how so?'

'Oh, Tom and Lizzie have gone off with a group of their friends . . . '

'And you did not wish to join them?'

'No,' said Sophie shortly.

Lady Isobel gave her a sidelong glance. 'Harry was not among the 'friends' I take it?'

'No,' answered Sophie again. 'Although I'm sure that would have made no difference to me.'

'I'm sure not,' agreed her mother, who appeared absorbed in sorting out the tangle of embroidery silks. She gave a sigh as she pulled a pink thread from a knot of blues and purples. 'I always knew, of course, that Tom would eventually marry Lizzie; they are ideally suited.'

Sophie's head shot up. 'Are they betrothed, then? Why does no one tell me anything?'

A chuckle escaped Lady Isobel. 'Hush, my love. No, there is no understanding as yet, but I am very sure there will be one before this summer is out.'

'But Tom is duty bound to marry for money. He told me so himself.'

'Tom exaggerates the matter. He imagines the Rubens has been sold. It has not! Along with some of the more valuable plate, it is safe in the bank. I am the one who had it copied. I am the one who had the plate put in the bank. Your stepfather is running low on funds, it's true, and from time to time he wonders aloud what this or that is worth. He did so with the Rubens, so I told him I thought it to be a copy.' She chuckled.

'He considers me to be a pretty, but empty-headed, fool . . . Believe me, Sophie, I am only foolish when it suits me. The only truly foolish act I committed was to take your stepfather as a husband, instead of a lover. An act I bitterly regret, but there is no reason why either Tom or you should suffer for that mistake.'

She sighed again. 'Yes, Tom and Lizzie will make an excellent match of it eventually. But you and Harry? I always perceived that would take a bit more doing.'

'Mama!' Sophie jumped from her seat.

'Oh, pray be seated Sophie, you are making me quite tired. Harry has been avoiding you — has he not?'

Dejectedly, Sophie sat down. 'Yes, it's no use your making plans, Mama — he hates me. He cannot bear to be with me. He hardly smiles in my direction, and when I ride over towards the Rectory, he pretends he hasn't seen me and kicks his horse to a gallop. Mama — it is so humiliating!'

'Foolish boy.' Lady Isobel smiled fondly. 'He has his pride, you see. So I'm afraid you have only one recourse.'

'Oh?' Sophie looked bewildered.

'Yes . . . You have to seduce him,' Lady Isobel said in a calm voice, as though instructing Sophie on the execution of the household accounts.

'Mama!' Sophie exclaimed in shocked tones.

Lady Isobel's eyebrows rose. 'Oh

don't 'Mama!' me. There is more to the art of seduction than mere body movements. You must seduce him with words. Now listen very carefully . . . '

★　★　★

Two days later, Sophie rose early. The morning was fresh and still; perfect weather for fishing.

Sure enough, when she reached it, a soft mist hung over the lake and the air was still and calm. Sophie dismounted from Firefly's back and led him across to the small jetty where Harry stood quietly with his fishing rod.

'Hello, Harry,' she said. 'I was beginning to think you were avoiding me.'

Harry looked far from pleased to see her. 'Not at all,' he said, his eyes fixed on the lake. 'Been busy, that's all.'

'I've missed you, Harry.'

'Yes, well . . . '

'You're meant to say — you've missed me too.'

'Hmm.'

'Anyway, Mama is wondering what you are about and wants you to dine with us soon. We've hardly seen you these last two weeks . . . Since the Highway robbery in fact.'

Harry put down his rod with a sigh. 'Yes, of course I'll come, Sophie, please tell your mother I'll be delighted — any time . . . '

'You were going to say 'but' something — I could hear it.'

Harry gave a groan. 'Well, if you must have it, Sophie . . . You know what we discussed the last time we were here? About not staying children for ever? Well, I've been doing some thinking, and you're right. We are grown up. I have no right to tell you that you shouldn't be alone with Julian when I spend time alone with you myself. It's no longer a good idea for us to do so. The fault is mine, I have been so used to treating you like a sister . . . but we can no longer go on easy in one another's company . . . '

'Why not?' asked Sophie moving as

close to him as she dared, but looking him straight in the eye, not upwards through her lashes as her mother had suggested.

'Because, well — because you are monstrous pretty, Sophie and it's hard on a fellow to have to be with you when he's not your brother.'

Sophie smiled. 'I have to tell you, Harry, you are not making a great deal of sense.'

Harry turned to face her and took her gently by the shoulders. 'You are Lady Sophia Ellington, young, pretty, with the whole world at your feet. I am plain Harry Crighton, son of a rector. The most I can hope for is a career in law, or the life of a gentleman farmer, Aunt Augusta willing, which I must confess I have more of a fancy for. Our paths are destined to be separate, as well you know.'

'You are under a misapprehension; the Ellingtons are not so very rich, Harry. Mama says we're merely custodians here at Ellington Place, duty bound to keep a large establishment in order to give others a livelihood. We are not so very extravagant. In fact, she has been teaching me in matters of economy. Candles, for example, are monstrous expensive, I could practise prodigious economies in that area. And I have had only one new riding habit in a year, and that only because this one grew too short and too tight. See, I have it on today. Can you not see how tight it is?'

Harry looked at her slender form, his eyes full of undisguised admiration.

Sighing he took a step backwards. 'It won't do, Sophie. You are a lady. The most I can aspire to is not good enough for you.'

So much for seduction, thought Sophie furiously. *How dare Harry turn her down?*

She took another step forward. 'Who are you to decide what's good enough for me? Am I to die an old maid for want of loving you?'

'Sophie, pray don't make this more

difficult than it is already. I've always known you'd grow up, go away and marry a Viscount or something. It was only when I realised you felt some kind of foolish notion to marry Julian, then found that you'd given him a lock of your hair, that I became so angry . . . And I shouldn't have done. I had no right, no right at all.'

'Well,' said Sophie consideringly. 'I did think I should maybe marry Julian and in that way I could stay near to Mama and Tom and my friends. Only I didn't realise then that it was you I wanted to be near to; you I didn't want to leave. Harry, I never loved Julian, that was just a silly notion of mine . . . You know, because of the poetry . . . Just think — he said once that my skin was like dew-soaked alabaster!'

Harry smiled. 'Really? I've never seen dew-soaked alabaster, myself.'

'I knew you would make fun.'

'Well, if it's poetry you want — your hair is the colour of sun-ripened corn at sunset.'

'Is it really?' Sophie asked, her eyes glowing.

'No idea. You'd better ask Julian.'

Sophie chuckled.

'I see you are determined to make me hate you, but you won't. I know what it is. You consider me a trollop or something of that nature, because I gave the locket with my hair in it to Julian. I swear to you it was meant as a token of friendship — not a love token. Julian has never even kissed me, nor would I want him to . . . ' She stepped closer again until she could feel the heat of him next to her.

This time Harry did not step away. 'Sophie — don't tempt me,' he groaned, looking down at her upturned face.

Sophie's eyes sparkled. 'Ah, so you would like, at least, to ravish me and I think I would very much enjoy being ravished by you — but, you refuse to marry me? Perhaps, then, you could be my secret lover? Well, I have an exceedingly good idea. I could marry

Julian after all! Then, because you live so close, you could easily be my secret love ... My handsome Highwayman ravisher! Just think of it!'

'You go too far, Sophie. This is not a joke!'

Turning away from the tender exasperation in Harry's eyes, Sophie was aware that for all her funning she was near to tears. 'I know,' she whispered in a shaky voice. 'I'm not good enough for you, Harry, am I? I'm too stupid to be a farmer's wife. Oh, I dare say I could practise economy and learn to make butter. I could look after the horses and I wouldn't mind wearing old clothes. But you don't love me enough, do you? That's really what it comes down to?'

A pair of strong hands landed on her shoulders. 'Don't love you? Sophie — I do nothing but love you, every minute of every day.'

'Well, that's not enough, Harry — obviously!'

Harry groaned, pulled her towards

him and kissed her hungrily. The kiss travelled from her lips down and down to a secret place inside her, which stirred and leapt. Shaken, she stepped away from him but her bruised lips curved into a smile. 'If this is what ravishing is — I must confess I like it exceedingly . . . You have to marry me now, don't you, Harry? You've quite ruined my reputation.'

'I will be put down as a fortune hunter and you as a hussy.'

'Well, I'm sorry to disappoint but Felix has likely spent my 'fortune'. I only have my sapphires and everyone knows they were stolen by an audacious Highwayman — were they not?'

'Lady Isobel would never allow such a match.'

'She will,' Sophie assured him demurely. 'I've asked her already and Tom thinks it's a capital idea.'

Slowly, Harry's face relaxed and a smile started in his eyes and spread to his mouth. 'Well then, Sophie, it seems you have it all worked out. All I have to do is ask you to marry me.'

'Oh, yes please,' said Sophie. 'And can we please also practise some more ravishing?'

THE END